BIKE ROCK

A Pedro the Water Dog Saves the Planet Primer

AVIS KALFSBEEK

PREQUEL SHORT STORY

Get a free Short Story prequel, Max's Holy Ride, at www.aviskalfsbeek.com/Max

Acknowledgements:
Benjamin Katz Creative ~ Patreon Patrons
Julian Hanna, The Manifesto Handbook
The Great American Rail Trail ~ Burning Man

ISBN 978-1-7355613-6-3 (First Edition Hardback)
ISBN 978-1-7355613-7-0 (First Edition Paperback)
ISBN 978-1-7355613-8-7 (Ebook)

www.AvisKalfsbeek.com

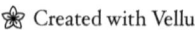 Created with Vellum

CHAPTER 1

PANNIER: A BASKET, BAG, OR BOX CARRIED IN PAIRS EITHER SLUNG OVER THE BACK OF A BEAST OF BURDEN OR ATTACHED TO THE SIDES OF A BICYCLE

On a crisp spring day, in a land of polar bears, beluga whales, and bright red salmon that return to their birthplace on a dime, a blue glacier wall glows in the distance. In a modern time when many say the earth will eventually not sustain human life, two riders on a tandem bike pull a double-kayak trailer on a winding road along a crystal clear bay with steep mountain peaks beyond.

Tilly, a young woman in her late twenties, wholesomely pretty, strong, with long black hair and an olive complexion, climbs into a kayak and paddles into the bay behind Liam as their lone green tent becomes a speck on the shore. They see Sitka spruce, western hemlock, and tall cedar trees along the coast as they paddle closer and closer to the 350-foot wall of ice.

"I'm so happy that I got to see the tiny fishing town where you grew up," Tilly says.

Liam smiles. "I know this was a bit of a trek from there, but I'm happy we made it." Liam is an athletic young man with short curly hair and clear blue eyes.

"It would have been a crime to come to Alaska and not see a glacier. I've lived in the north forever, but I've never seen one until today."

They are silent as they take in the beauty.

"Words can't describe it," Tilly says reverently.

They paddle in synchronized rhythm looking up at the impressive glacier.

"I've been thinking about my next race," Tilly says.

"Where to next, my dear?"

"That's just it. I'd like to take a break."

Liam is surprised. "Why?"

"I know what you are thinking. Well, what your dad would be thinking, anyway. That it's because I didn't win in Kona."

"Are you kidding? We would both be thinking that would make you want to race even more."

Tilly smiles. "I would really like to take a break. Swim and run just for fun. Spend some more time with Camas and the One More Year and Refill projects."

Liam looks a little hurt.

"And with you, of course!"

He brightens.

"I also thought that it could be your turn. You competed in swimming before you met me."

"You know, there is a race in July I've always wanted to do. It crosses the International Date Line from Finland to Sweden."

"Well, there you have it. You'll have a little less than a year to prepare. That's perfect."

"Thank you," Liam says sweetly as they paddle closer to the glacier.

"I'm only sorry that P is sailing with Moore and won't be able to coach you for several months."

Liam laughs. "I'll have to get by with you." He paddles ahead and turns his boat around and floats up next to Tilly so they are facing each other side by side. He reaches out and holds onto her kayak.

"Whatcha' doin'? Need a kiss?" Tilly flirts.

"I thought we'd celebrate. I brought something. It's on ice."

Liam pulls out a bottle of champagne and two glass flutes.

"Wow! Aren't you full of surprises!"

Liam unfastens the cage and slowly twists the bottle around the cork with his strong hands. Just as the champagne opens with a gentle pop, a large piece of heavy ice falls from the glacier into the sea, large waves crashing up upon the glacier wall, creating rhythmic waves in the distance.

They laugh, eyes wide in awe. Liam pours the champagne and hands Tilly a glass.

"Thank you." She holds up the glass. "It's so beautiful in this light with the glacier behind. The falling ice is beautiful too, but so bittersweet." She starts to lift the glass to her mouth.

"Wait, I want to make a toast." Liam holds up his glass. "From the moment I saw you swimming in the lake, and you turned around to scold me, I knew I wanted to travel the world with you. Travel far to places like this and places near, like our back yard. You care about people, and you care about this planet and things like glaciers. You seem to care about me too."

Tilly has tears in her eyes.

Liam pulls out a ring box, opens it, and takes a ring out of it. "Tilly DeMontagne, will you marry me?"

More tears fall as Tilly reaches out over the boats and

hugs Liam, tipping over their glasses. The champagne bottle falls into the water.

"Oh no, I'm sorry! Yes, yes! I'll marry you!" she calls out as she hugs and kisses him.

Liam puts the ring on her left ring finger. "Are you crying out of joy, for the iceberg, or for the lost champagne?"

Tilly looks into his eyes lovingly. "I guess all three."

Liam laughs. "Well, yes, it was a $300 bottle, but you don't have to worry. I told great uncle Bill that I was proposing, and he sent us with a couple of bottles. We'll have one back at the tent."

"Can Bill stop the glacier from receding too?" Tilly kisses Liam, "Liam Selkirk, I love you, and not just for the champagne!"

CHAPTER 2

CASSETTE: A COLLECTION OF GEARS THAT IS ATTACHED TO THE REAR WHEEL ON MOST MODERN BICYCLES

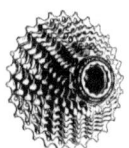

L oud rock music plays in the do-it-yourself Sandglass Movers and Makers Studio. Various artists and craftspeople work with metal, glass, lasers, pottery, 3-D printers, sewing machines, and other tools in a large warehouse bustling with creative energy.

Camas, a young woman in her twenties, with curly, strawberry blond hair, freckles, a fit full-figure and one arm decorated in artistic tattoos, is skimpily clad in an elaborate costume of feathers, steampunk goggles, tulle, sequins, and lace-up knee-high boots. She leans over an old bicycle, her voluptuous cleavage bulging out of her sexy feathered bra top. Various men and a couple of women pay appreciating notice. Graeme, Liam's father, who is in his early fifties with a rugged handsomeness, walks past and is merely curious.

"Hey, Camas," he says with raised eyebrows.

"Graeme, what's up? What are you working on?"

"It's a surprise. Something for the wedding."

"Those two crazy kids. I told them that marriage is for sissies."

"Maybe."

Graeme examines her bike. "What in the hell is that?"

"I'm putting a bike together for the big day. Needs lights and some flash. Thought I'd try on one of my costumes too." She twirls in place. "At least they're tying the knot at the biggest party on the planet."

"How'd they swing that anyway? It's nearly impossible to get big groups in now."

"Wow. Mr. Selkirk is in the know on Burning Man," Camas teases.

"Just sayin'."

"Josh and I were planning to go anyway. We pitched One More Year as an art project. They're also using the WowFlo refill stations."

"Is it an art project?"

"The One More Year billboards are art and the thousands of posts of people showing their old stuff and not buying new stuff is right up their artsy alley. *Communal effort* is one of their ten principals."

"Your chain is loose. Let me fix that."

"Hey, thanks. I heard you donated an entire section of this maker's studio for bike repair. That's swell of you. You just might be turning into a nice guy."

"Ugh," Graeme grunts as he continues fixing Camas's chain. "Just helping the people keep their stuff longer."

CHAPTER 3
CAGE: THE PREFERRED FANCY NAME FOR WATER BOTTLE HOLDER

A peregrine falcon takes flight from a steep, rocky mountain ledge into a deep blue sky. From the soaring view of the falcon, from a very long distance, a speck of color appears in a vast expanse of unending desert. Suddenly, the falcon dives 200 miles per hour to the dry earth, much too fast for the naked eye to see it catch the rodent in its talons. Passing across the beautifully patterned desert land, a rattlesnake is coiled and rattling. The barren, cracked earth continues mile after mile, a deep blue sky overhead. A single, brightly colored Moroccan tent appears, its luxuriousness in stark contrast to the Black Rock playa's barrenness.

Inside, a diverse group of six people sits around a large table with an eight-foot square map in the center. Maximo, a very short, handsome, rugged, charismatic man of Italian descent, in his mid-thirties with long, silky, dark hair, leans over the map with a colored pencil. He wears traditional East Indian clothing, bracelets, and an emerald green silk headband. Max heads the civic planning and tech aspects of Burning Man and is the unspoken eldest of the elders, not in years but karmic evolution. A beautiful blend of the feminine energy of peacefulness paired with a warrior, jump-into-action strength allows him to oversee the desert city. Occasional use of psychedelics in a sacred ancient shaman-like practice is of help to him as well.

Rajikaru, a tall, slender, Asian man with grey hair in a stylish blunt bob, dressed in a new wave David-Byrne-like light blue linen grand-dad collared shirt as sleek as his frame, sits across the table, "There's no way in hades we can disallow vehicles into Black Rock City!"

"Never say never, " Max responds.

"Man, there are so many of the principals that just would not live on."

"Which?"

"Well, radical self-reliance for one. How do they bring their shit in? Radical self-expression for another? How do they bring in all of what makes their experience? The gifting, the costumes, their elaborate homes away from home."

"We've thought about this on and off before, and we've always agreed it's not possible," says Shasta, a strong, tattooed-everywhere woman with a crew cut and piercings, wearing long shorts and combat boots. "It would be a logistical impossibility."

"Yes, impossible," Sharu repeats.

"That's not correct on two points," Max says respectfully and thoughtfully. "Yes, we agreed not to proceed with it because of our consensus guidelines that have always worked. Everyone participates, and we all must agree before moving forward. This has taken some things longer to move ahead, but it has worked for us. Regarding disallowing motors, I agreed to table it in the past because the time was not right."

Max pauses, stands, pushes aside the silk tent door, and looks out upon the expanse of desert.

"And the second?" Shasta says impatiently.

"The second point that is not correct is that it would be logistically imposs..."

"Oh, my goddess," Karu interrupts, "How can you say that?" Realizing he has interrupted, he says, "Max, I'm sorry, go on."

"We know that nothing is impossible," Samprati, a black woman in her mid-forties with long hair and a strong, voluptuous body, wearing khakis, boots, a *One More Year* T-shirt, and a bandana around her neck, says confidently.

"Karu, would you agree with that?" Max asks, looking him squarely in the eye from across the room.

Karu doesn't respond. He shakes his head, stands, and places his fingers extended on the table as he leans over the large map.

Max walks slowly over to Karu, picks up a Moroccan pouf cushion, places it in front of him, and steps onto it. Now they are eye to eye.

"If we decide that an experience on the playa without cars is impossible, how will the world ever do it? Would you agree that it is not impossible? Not that we are moving forward with it. Just that it is still on the table?"

Karu pauses. He sighs. "Yes," Karu says reluctantly.

Max hugs Karu, then leaps playfully off of the pouf, skipping around the table to embrace each of the others. Music plays, and Max grabs Plume's hand. Plume, a young woman in her twenties with long hair, wears a flowing skirt, spaghetti strap camisole, daisy-chain headband, many bracelets, and large round rose-colored glasses. They begin to dance skillfully in an expressive ecstatic dance style.

Max dances over to the table. He talks excitedly with Plume, Samprati, and Shasta, pointing to parts of the map.

CHAPTER 4

REAR VIEW MIRROR: A REFLECTIVE SURFACE OF GLASS COATED WITH METAL AMALGAM, MOUNTED IN A POSITION USUALLY ON HANDLEBARS TO SEE THE VIEW BEHIND

A five-year-old boy with short brown hair and a backpack rides his bicycle down a neighborhood street. He stops at a stop sign. A car to his right stops and waits for him to cross. He continues riding down the road, his school a block away in the distance. A giant Hummer travels behind him, driven by a blond woman with large sunglasses.

"Of course, I'm closing it down. It's a useless pile of rocks with a river 6,000 feet below. We're leaving a bit of it for the Indians and green-heads."

Goosey Bitumines, early thirties, wearing big costume and diamond jewelry, a silk top and jeans, travels over the speed limit as she talks on her phone, distracted. The Hummer bears down towards the boy, then blows by with just an inch between the metal of her rig and the bike. Surprised, Jack jerks his head, then swerves to hit the curb and falls hard. He begins to cry.

Ella, a pretty woman of Austrian-German descent in her

mid-thirties with short blonde hair, and her young daughter are on bikes, see the incident and stop to help. Ella leans down to help Jack up and sees his arm is bleeding.

"Hey, come back! Come back, you careless disaster gas-guzzling road hog! Dummes Stück Scheiße!" *stupid piece of shit* in German, Ella says with a vertical swinging arm movement. She looks at her daughter and the boy.

"Sorry for the swearing. Jack, are you OK?"

"How in the world did we let Camas talk us into getting married at Burning Man?" Tilly says as she and Liam ride their town bikes across the Long Bridge towards Sandglass, with colorful sailboats on shimmering Lake Bijou Nez in the distance.

"She's persuasive."

"Yes, she is."

They ride on with cars whirring by on the bridge.

Tilly's face looks pained. She stops abruptly and closes her eyes, her face in a grimace.

She sees a flash of a couple riding on a windy lakeside road with cars passing.

Liam stops.

"Are you OK? What's wrong."

Tilly opens her eyes, shakes it off. "It's nothing."

"Are you sure?" Liam touches her hand.

"Yes. I did want to tell you that I got a call from a woman in Napa asking me to help her with a project."

"What kind of project?"

"Something to do with bikes. She saw the One More Year billboards and thought I might help."

"She'd be fortunate to have it."

Tilly kisses Liam. They get back on the bikes and ride on.

"Those sailboats make me miss Moore and P," Tilly says.

"I'm sure they're having a wonderful time."

Tilly's black curly water dog, Pedro, harnessed to a 35 foot monohull sailboat, looks bravely out into a massive rainstorm crossing the Atlantic Ocean. Spit, a young man in his twenties, with a surfer-vibe, and wet blond hair to his shoulders, is in a raincoat, throwing up over the side. Anika, Spit's girlfriend, a 6'2" beautiful, athletic, black Belgian young woman runs around the boat confidently helping Tilly's brother, captain Moore, at the helm.

"Ella, Thank you again for helping Jack," Martha says, standing in her kitchen.

Jack does schoolwork at the kitchen counter.

"I've just had it with this town! It's just a matter of time until the accident causes death. You heard those poor newlyweds got hit by the truck last summer while they were on their honeymoon, right? Dead." Ella says, frustrated.

"Oh my god. That's right."

"It was a wine packaging truck, they said, but it could have been anyone. There was no bike lane."

"So scary."

"I've asked the mayor to speak with us next Monday night. I'm inviting other mothers from the school to meet at the school auditorium."

"I'll be there!"

CHAPTER 5

BOTTOM BRACKET: A COLLECTION OF BALL BEARINGS AND SPINDLE HOUSED WITHIN THE BOTTOM BRACKET SHELL OF THE FRAME

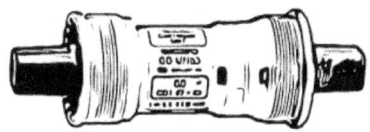

"**A**nd why are we on the train to Calgary again?" Camas asks Tilly in the Amtrak dining car, pine trees and steep mountains framing the tracks.

"You asked me what I wanted to do for a bachelorette party, and this is it?"

"Most girls want to wear a penis crown in Las Vegas."

Passengers turn to look at Camas.

"What is *it* exactly?" Camas asks.

"Three things. I want to spend some time with my best friend. I want to get caught up on One More Year and the Refill project. You've kicked ass on that, by the way."

"Thanks, sista. They're your projects."

"They're *our* projects. You've been running herd as the CFO."

"There have been some chief F-offs like when I called the largest billboard company in the U.S. and told them they should give us space for free."

"Well, you've taken to it like a duck to water."

"Quack. What's three?"

"We're meeting an old friend. He's someone who knows the ins and outs of the energy world."

"OK, OK, now we're getting to it. What's in your craw now?"

"I got a call from a woman who wants to change her town into a bike town. There've been some deaths from cars hitting people on bikes. You've heard me talk about it before. The national parks are being attacked by big oil. They reduced Bear's Ears by 85 percent and Grand Staircase by 50 percent, and now they're threatening to start uranium mining again at the Grand Canyon!"

"What's the goal with this guy?"

"I'm not sure. I just need to understand more about what's happening."

"Well, it might have been nice to know about number three before leaving. I brought sexy bachelorette party outfits, not sabotage-a-mine-wear."

"I've told you always to come prepared," Tilly teases.

"Ticket sales are off," Sharu says to Max and Plume as they walk to meet the other elders for the Golden Spike ceremony marking the center of Black Rock City.

"We anticipated that," Max responds.

"How off?" Plume asks.

"About thirty percent."

"We've wanted to get back to basics for some time now. Less of an Instagram photo experience and back to being present for each other. People are still thinking through how they'll make it happen, and then sales will pick up."

"How can they feel radical self-reliance if they can't leave the place on their own?" Sharu asks as the three arrive at the ceremony.

"We'll get them in here, and we'll get them out. They'll need to trust. Trust in themselves to pare down their Burning Man belongings to what's essential. They'll still have generators. They'll still have ebikes if they need oomf. They just won't have a personal vehicle or a monstrous RV."

"They'll be more connected to the land," Plume agrees softly.

CHAPTER 6

BIKE GREASE: WATERPROOF LUBRICATION WHICH IS GENERALLY USED IN METAL-TO-METAL PLACES ON THE BIKE YOU DON'T TAKE APART OR SEE TOO OFTEN

"**B**ring me up to date on One More Year and Refill, Bill."

Beautiful vistas of grassy meadows and wildflowers with tall mountains in the distance pass by the train car window.

Camas points to her Macbook screen. "Ember came through on her commitment in Kona, so we have 49 billboards up across the US, Canada, and Europe and 16 more going up in the next few months. We're raising money to get into more cities and countries. We have commitments from a third of Fortune 500 businesses, 52 percent of colleges and universities, 24 percent of cities, and 13 states to be 100 percent refillers and to tax plastic water bottles within five years."

Tilly hugs Camas. "That's so exciting, Cam!"

The train comes around a bend, and in the distance, there are miles upon miles of oil drilling rigs pumping slowly up and down. It is barren and grey.

"Holy shit! It looks like a scene from battle for middle-earth," Camas says.

"I don't think anyone's winning that battle."

Glistening, glittery high rises of downtown Calgary tower over clean city streets with trendy shops and restaurants. Camas and Tilly walk into a hip restaurant with white table-cloths and fresh flowers. The host leads them to a table where Rock, a tall, handsome man in his fifties, with a long handlebar mustache and hazel-brown eyes, is standing by a table waiting to greet them.

"Tilly!" he says as he kisses her on the cheek.

"Hi Rock," Tilly says warmly "This is Camas."

Camas shakes his hand perfunctorily.

"Hi, Camas. Ladies, please sit," he says with a gentle southern drawl.

Tilly and Camas sit across from Rock.

"Thanks for meeting us here. I know Calgary is not very close to Texas."

"It's no problem. I knew it was easier for you to get here, and I scheduled some meetings."

The waiter arrives. "May I bring you wine or a cocktail?"

"I'll have a shot of tequila and a Kokanee, please," Camas says.

"A girl after my own heart. I'll have the same. Make it Pasion Azteca Anejo."

Camas is perturbed. "Change that to a mezcal."

"I'll have a Kombucha, please," Tilly requests.

"After that long train ride, you're not drinking?" Camas questions.

"We'll be drinking later, I expect."

"True."

"You took the train? How was that?" Rock asks.

"Beautiful except for those oil fields," Tilly answers.

"Yes, it is industrial. You look great, Tilly."

"Thanks, Rock. You do too."

They smile at each other. Tilly looks away. Camas looks more perturbed.

"So we're here to ask you some oil questions," Camas says forcefully. "Tilly says you're a big oil guy."

"My company focuses on energy, yes. All types of energy."

"But oil is in the mix," Camas presses.

"Sure, yes."

Tilly nudges Camas under the table, "I let Camas know a tiny bit about you."

"Like the fact that you're rich."

"Life has been good to me."

"Rich from oil?"

"Cam," Tilly says, raising her eyebrows pointedly. "Rock, what she means is do you know how the oil industry works?"

"I would say that I have a good command of that knowledge, yes."

The waiter brings the drinks.

"Saved by the tequila!"

CHAPTER 7

SPOKES: SMALL RADIATING BARS INSERTED IN THE HUB OF A WHEEL TO SUPPORT THE RIM

"Welcome to the Golden Spike Ceremony," Max says. "Today, as usual, the spokes of Black Rock City will be laid out by our talented surveying team."

Sharu, Samprati, Plume, and Shasta stand on either side of Max, and a group of about fifty people, volunteers, and a few bystanders, stand around an area marked by the crossing of two taut strings staked low to the ground.

Max notices a woman pull out her phone and start to film. He walks over to her.

"Hello. Why are you filming?" He asks gently.

"I'm with KRNV television station in Reno."

"I'm sorry, we don't film this. This is a sacred ritual."

"Won't it help promote your festival?"

"Perhaps, but its spirit will be destroyed if taken out of context by a camera lens."

"Oh," she says, disappointed, putting her camera away.

"I welcome you to stay," Max says, then walks back to stand in between the elders.

"This year, the wheel of time expands. We'll be surveying to extend roads to transport supplies and then mark the paths for burners to arrive on bicycles or foot. We celebrate this commitment to honor and protect this land in this ritual of beginnings."

Samprati hands Max the hammer. "Here is the exact center of Black Rock City. Today signifies the starting point of the building of our city in the desert, both the physical and that which cannot be seen. Let us close our eyes. I won't close my eyes when I use the sledgehammer."

The crowd laughs.

"Feel in your heart the spirit with which we honor all who have gone before us and all who will follow. May our intentions be true, so with our hands and hearts, we can create a new home from the dust and return it to dust."

Max hits the stake into the center of the strings. The crowd opens their eyes and cheers. Max hands the sledgehammer to Samprati.

"Today, I bring *immediacy* and *participation* to the city and this moment."

Sharu takes the hammer. "Today, I bring *radical self-expression* and *radical inclusion* to the city and this moment." He hands the hammer to Shasta.

"Today, I bring *civic responsibility* and *leave no trace* to the city and this moment," Shasta says.

Plume takes the hammer, "Today, I bring *gifting* and *decommodification* to the city and this moment."

"And today, I bring *communal effort* and *radical self-reliance* to the city and this moment," Max says proudly.

Samprati hands Max a bottle of champagne.

"We baptize our new Black Rock City with those here entrusted to build another wheel of time, the hub for all things to come, where this spike and the center of the spokes will become the burning man that shoots a spark into the hearts that attend."

He crashes the bottle on the spike. The group cheers.

"Now, go build Bike Rock City!"

Sharu shakes his head.

CHAPTER 8

STEM: THE PART THAT CONNECTS THE HANDLEBAR TO THE FRAME

An elegant, well-heeled man and woman are seated at the table across from Tilly, Camas, and Rock. The man wears a designer suit. Camas looks over and eyes the woman's extremely large diamond ring and haute couture dress.

"I can sure see the oil in this fancy town. Do you know how the money side of the business works too?" Camas asks.

"I've been involved in most of the major energy deals in one way or another over the past twenty-five years, so yes."

"Thanks for being so open," Tilly says.

Rock smiles at her. He looks at Camas, "Is there a certain question, in particular, you would like to ask?"

Camas looks awkward, suddenly not so confident. She turns to Tilly, "What's our question again?"

"If there was suddenly no more use of cars in the United States, or Canada for that matter, what would happen?"

Rock looks very surprised. Shoots back his tequila.

Goosey is sitting behind a large desk with a view of the St. Louis, Missouri, skyline outside her floor-to-ceiling office window.

"Good marnin', sweet thing? How was Napa?" her father, Sherman Bitumines, says on the other end of the line. His voice is low and distinguished, and he pronounces his *or*'s as *ar*.

"It was fabulous as usual, papa."

"What are you doing?"

"We've got the shareholder conference call tomorrow morning, remember?"

"Yes, I do. Are you prepared?"

"No sweat," Goosey responds, looking at her long fingernails.

"Unless they bring up the god damn Grand Canyon or what's that thing again... oh yes, climate."

"Oh, papa, don't you worry. You know I can always smooth it out. As long as they're making money, that's all just lip service."

"Sounds like a piece of cake."

"Let them eat cake." Goosey laughs without smiling.

"You may have read that approximately one-fifth of greenhouse gases comes from cars. So if there were no more cars, there would be that much less CO_2."

"What would happen to the oil companies?" Tilly asks.

"That's a good question. About a third of global oil demand is from cars, so it is not the least bit inconsequential. Some oil, gas, and coal companies are owned by governments or private owners, but about a fifth are owned by shareholders."

"What does that have to do with anything?" Camas asks impatiently.

"He's telling us Camas."

Their food arrives. Camas flirts with the waiter.

"Go on then," Camas says as she takes a big bite.

"Shareholders look for stability. If things look shaky for any reason, including uncertainty about the future, fewer will be willing to buy, and that makes the share price go down."

"Are oil investments shaky?" Tilly asks.

"Well, this town is a good example. One of the leaders of the petroleum association of Canada said that 'due to an unrelenting focus on climate action during the federal election, the uncertainty was dragging down the oilpatch.'"

"Basically, the climate platforms of the candidates created uncertainty for investors?" Tilly asks.

"Exactly."

"No comprendo," Camas says with food in her mouth.

Tilly explains patiently, "Let's say that the only reason you drink mezcal is the worm."

"Damn right."

"...and one day, your favorite worm-mezcal producer lets you know that some bottles will have the worm, but some might not because the climate has caused a die-off of worms."

"Does it always have to be about the climate?"

Tilly rolls her eyes. "Would you still buy the mezcal?"

"No. Too risky."

"So that's what Rock is saying about the oil. The investors buy the shares to make money, and to make money there needs to be the worm which in this case is a stable demand for oil."

"I think I get it."

"You do, silly."

"Not only that, electric cars are trending to take a big bite out of oil business," Rock explains. "They make up one percent of new car sales now and are expected to reach thirty percent by 2040. Add to that, of the six basic indicators of share stability, oil has three precarious ones: government policy, technological changes, and extreme weather fluctuations. That gets from a newly paved road to quicksand pretty darn fast."

"What are the other three?" Camas asks.

"Wars, inflation, and how well the company itself is performing."

"We certainly don't need another war or inflation, but if we could make sure investors knew if a corporation wasn't performing, that might be a tipping point."

"I've always loved your brain."

Camas turns her head away to hide her grimace from his sugar sweetness. She pretends to reach for something and knocks Rock's water glass over onto him.

"Oh, so sorry," she says sarcastically. "I think it's time to go anyway."

Camas quickly stands up.

"Rock, why are you helping us?" Tilly asks.

"Let's just say that when I looked into the eyes of my grandson, without saying a word, just a 'goo' and a 'gah gah,' he asked me how I could forgive myself."

"Well, how can you?" Camas asks.

Tilly stands too and pulls Camas by her arm. "Time to go. Thank you so much for meeting us here."

Tilly hugs Rock.

He kisses her on the cheek. "Can I take you to dinner?"

"She's engaged," Camas says dryly. "We're outta here."

"Nice meeting you, Camas."

Tilly mouths, "I'm sorry," as they walk out of the restaurant.

"Hey, what was with you in there?"

"Just a 'goo' and a 'gah gah,' he asked me how I could forgive myself," Camas mocks.

"That was sweet."

"That dude has oil for blood. He ain't making no changes," Camas says with hip hop hand motions.

"Please don't speak in hip hop. You don't know that."

"Deeds not words, sista. Time will tell."

"True."

"Now, let's get this bachelorette party started!" Camas says as she unbuttons her blouse to reveal a sexy camisole. She reaches into her bag and pulls out high heels. "You need to have some fun before you're tied down."

Tilly hugs her and laughs. "Let's go!"

CHAPTER 9

NIPPLE: A SMALL FLANGED NUT THAT HOLDS A SPOKE IN PLACE ON THE RIM OF A WHEEL

A group of elementary school mothers and one father sit in chairs in a circle on a 1930's Spanish-style auditorium stage. They chat as mayor Dandy, wearing a short-brimmed Panama hat with a light blue grosgrain band, seersucker jacket, and jeans, walks down the auditorium aisle to join the group.

"I asked you here today to brainstorm about how to make our town safer for our kids on bikes. I've asked the mayor to join us and also invited Tilly DeMontagne to call in," Ella says.

"The triathlete?" a mom in the group asks.

Another mom answers, "Yes. She's the one who has the One More Year billboards."

"And helped the plastic refill bill too," another adds.

"Yes, that's right. Everyone OK with me joining her in?"

The group nods.

"Of course!"

"Yes," they say.

Ella opens and taps her laptop. "Hi Tilly, I'm here with some parents and mayor Dandy.

"Thanks for inviting me."

"Tilly, as I told you, we want to convert our town to a bike town. Martha's son was almost hit by an SUV last week. We don't want to worry about sending our kids off and getting hit."

Tilly turns away from the screen and has a pained face.

She sees a couple cycling on a windy lake road. A semi truck is traveling a bit down the road behind them.

"Tilly? Tilly, can you hear us?"

Tilly shakes the image from her mind. "Yes. I'm here! I'm so sorry to hear about that near accident. I don't have specific experience with bike changes in towns, but I'll do whatever I can to help."

"Could you lend your name to our efforts? If we could say you were involved, it might help us gain support," the mayor asks.

"Of course."

Tilly, Liam, and Camas share a bottle of Bijou Nez red wine on the winery's outdoor patio.

"They say we need to put your wedding in a box," Camas says.

"I don't know what you're talking about," Tilly responds.

Liam reads from his phone, "It says, each individual's things must fit into a 48 x 48 harvest crate."

"That seems fine."

"Fine for you. You wear the same two things every day."

"Hey!" Tilly laughs.

"And those two things look lovely on you," Liam says.

Tilly kisses Liam.

"How am I going to fit all of my costumes and the wedding present and my rockin' the kasbah lair decor and the necklaces I'm going to bring as my gifting. They're holographic images of my breasts, by the way."

Liam raises his eyebrows and laughs.

"Don't encourage her." Tilly turns to Camas, "That sounds like MOOP."

"How could my boobs be matter out of place?"

A winery guest at the table next to them looks over at Camas's breasts.

Camas looks down at her breasts. "There's always a place for my boobs. I'm not going to be able to be everywhere at once with my nakedness, so my boobs will be."

"Huh?" Tilly says skeptically, smiling. "Are you going to be naked at the wedding?"

Camas teases, "Is that a problem?"

"Maybe for my dad," Liam says.

"What about bikes and power?" Camas asks.

"It says one bike and one generator can reside outside the cube." Liam reads from his phone.

"Thank goddess!"

CHAPTER 10

CHAINRINGS: GEARS THAT ARE ATTACHED TO THE RIGHT-HAND CRANK ARM NEARER TO THE FRONT OF THE BIKE

Streams of exuberant, beautifully costumed Burning Man attendees of all ages ride bikes down wide marked dirt corridors from the outer edge of the playa toward Black Rock City. People travel on hoverboards, tandem bikes, large moving art bikes, e-bikes, single speed fixies, small scooters, and foot.

The Golden Gate Bridge frames the backdrop of a vast parking lot full of electric-powered buses. Volunteers help burners in costumes load bikes and cubes in one electric shuttle, then direct them to another area to load onto their passenger shuttle. Other attendees travel through the welcome arch of the Biggest Little City in the World, Reno, to park their vehicle in a lot to be transferred by e-bus to the playa. Several hundred burners, travel as far as they are permitted, to a large lot in Gerlach, population 107, and according to the town's welcome sign, the Center of the Known Universe, the last stop for vehicles.

On the outskirts of the playa, burners exit electric shuttles laughing, dancing, and singing along to the loud, energetic electric dance music. Camas exits a shuttle in a costume of feathers, turquoise-glass steampunk goggles, hot pants tucked into tall platform lace boots, with sparkling beads on her forehead and décolletage. Her boyfriend, Josh, athletic, black, in his late 20's, with a beard, exits next wearing a tartan kilt, combat boots, and a sleeveless T-shirt that is bedazzled with *It's good to be black on the moon.* Tilly steps out next, wearing a simple light green linen tunic dress with leather boots. She has peacock feathers and beads tied into her long black hair. Liam exits wearing a poseidon-aquaman-merman-inspired costume with a blue feather and shell crown, fins on his forearms and calves, fish scale bike shorts, and water shoes with scales. Shimmering paint covers his bare muscular torso. They all wear Camas's naked boob necklaces.

"Wow, look at all of these bikes," Tilly says as she watches the burners ride off towards the city.

Camas holds her phone up to a scanner held by a volunteer, then pulls her decorated bike off of the shuttle. Cubes of belongings and generators are delivered directly to camps by the e-shuttles.

"Where are your bikes?" Camas asks.

"My dad said..."

"Here it is!" Graeme calls as he walks up with a white tandem bike. Elaborate lights and metal heart cutouts decorate the wheels. Liz, Graeme's girlfriend, an attractive, slender woman in her late forties, with shoulder-length auburn hair with a few strands of grey, walks beside him. Graeme wears a colorful One More Year cycling jersey and bike shorts, and Liz wears an artistic furry alpaca hat at the top of a long neck, a fur bra, fur hotpants, and leather boots.

"It's an early wedding present from Liz and me."

"Wow, thanks. That's awesome," Tilly says hugging them. "Great costume, Liz!"

Tilly climbs onto the front seat.

"Hey, I wanted the front," Liam teases. "Thanks, Dad and Liz!"

"Hey Graeme, cool bike, but isn't that just your bike jersey," Camas says as she hugs Graeme hello.

"I'm part of the One More Year art installation," Graeme says as he smiles and takes their bikes off the shuttle.

The group rides off toward Black Rock City, blending into the mass movement of burners spinning into an alternate reality.

Ana Chronism, an elegant and striking woman in her thirties, with a gently curled brunette bob and snow-white skin, exits the shuttle dramatically, head high, shoulders back, in the most extraordinary 1940's-era Esther Williams-inspired swimsuit along with a crown and clear plastic thigh-high boots. Topper Martinez, Ana's partner, early forties, muscular, with dark hair in a crew cut, wearing tight glitter shorts, suspenders, a top hat and platform boots, shows his ticket and pulls a rickshaw bike off of the shuttle. Ana climbs gracefully onto the back with her phone in her hand and sits down.

"Those sons of bitches," she says in a regal Greta Garbo-esque voice.

"What's wrong, my dear?"

"The record company delayed the album release. I'm so fed up with that misogynistic music plantation."

"Let's have fun."

"I'll try," she says morosely.

CHAPTER 11
HEADSET: THE COLLECTION OF BEARINGS HOUSED WITHIN THE HEAD TUBE OF THE FRAME, PROVIDING SMOOTH STEERING

Napa visions a clothed bike city as the anti-consumerism message of the One More Year art installation feels quite at home in this nearly-nude no-*moop montage*.

Tilly, Camas, Liam, and Josh set up the One More Year art installation, a life size 14' x 48' billboard that reads *One More Year, keep your stuff longer people*, which is 12 feet from the ground with a dancing platform in front of it. At the bottom is an open-air tent equipped with iPads where burners share stuff they've owned a long time. A scantily clad man types *1967 feather boa, Club Fuggazi, Jamie Freewheel*.

Ella stands in front of a large group of parents and teachers at Back to School night. She passes out 'Let's create a bike town to keep our kids safe!' flyers to the crowd from the basket on her bicycle.

Tilly, Liam, Camas, Josh, Graeme, and Liz explore magical Burning Man. Transformational experiences ranging from sexy to psychedelic, intimate to gargantuan, impactful to comical, intellectual to spiritual bring them closer to each other and their global-mystic community.

Tilly and Camas sit cross-legged in front of their tents meditating. Tilly has her eyes closed, sitting peacefully, and doesn't see Camas handing out boob necklaces to passersby.

Mayor Dandy stands at the podium of a Napa City Council meeting and shows a video of Utrecht and its mastermind web of bike lanes.

Camas and Liz decorate the One More Year tent in simple wedding décor of large white paper flowers. Tilly sets a framed photo of her and Liam on bicycles on the guest book table.

CHAPTER 12

FORK: THE TWO-LEGGED PART OF THE FRAME THAT HOLDS THE FRONT WHEEL IN PLACE

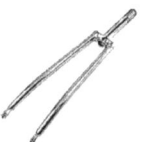

Dust begins to rise as a wind storm heads toward Black Rock City. Burners pull scarves up around their noses and mouths and put on their goggles. In the distance, the colossal burning man structure glows through the dust.

"It's bad luck to see the bride before the wedding. I'm spending the night at Camas's tent. Josh is going to sleep in a tent near you. I'll see you in the morning. I'm going to hit the hay."

Liam has a pouty face.

Tilly kisses him. "OK. You can at least give me a ride back. Sure hope the storm ends by tomorrow."

Liam helps Tilly with her goggles and face covering and pulls his on too. People are moving quickly on bikes and running toward cover.

Liam climbs on the front seat of the bike with Tilly behind. They begin to make their way back to their camp through a chaotic scene of people and bicycles. Suddenly, a large art-mobile appears out of the dust.

Tilly has a pained face and closes her eyes. *A man and a*

woman cycle on a winding lake road. They go around a large curve. A semi truck with a load of logs is behind them. It starts to pass without much room, with a loud whir of the engine and tires. Another logging truck comes from the other direction, partially in their lane. A screech of brakes.

A large art vehicle honks loudly. Tilly screams, opens her eyes, and begins to cry hysterically.

"I can't do it."

"It's OK, my love. I'm being careful. It's OK," Liams says as he gets off the bike and puts his arms around her.

"I can't do it. I can't marry you." Tilly sobs into his shoulder.

Liam rides the tandem bike out of Black Rock City with hundreds of other departing Burning Man attendees. He the tandem bike. The back seat is empty.

Liam and Graeme sit on the e-shuttle returning home.

"She just needs time," Graeme says, putting his hand on Liam's.

"I don't know dad. She seemed pretty sure about it."

"She is strong."

"I guess I'll focus on my swim race training."

Liam sits quietly, looking out the window.

"Tilly told me about the town that wants to get rid of cars. I told her I'd go to Utrecht to get a copy of their city plan and meet with some people. Liz has some meetings there, so we're making a trip out of it."

Liam is silent.

"Your dad knows how to swim, you know."

"Yes, I know."

"Why don't you come with me and you can train there?"

"That's OK, Dad. Thanks though. Too much jet fuel CO_2."

"And you don't want to be that far from Tilly."

"And I don't want to be that far from Tilly," Liam says sadly as he looks out the window.

CHAPTER 13

COG: A SINGLE GEAR ON A CASSETTE OR FREEWHEEL GEAR CLUSTER, OR THE SINGLE REAR GEAR ON A FIXED-GEAR BIKE

Tilly and Camas clean up the One More Year installation with volunteers. Camas opens her mouth to say something, then stops and continues working. She lifts her head to say something and stops herself again. She continues cleaning up.

She turns her head towards Tilly again, pretending to work.

"Oh, for crying out loud. Why don't you just say it," Tilly says.

"Say what?"

"Whatever it is you're not saying."

"What's that?" Camas looks innocent.

"We both know that the air is never silent when you're in the vicinity."

"Ouch."

"It's nothing bad. I love all of you."

"Well, maybe you just don't know all of me. Maybe I don't have anything to say."

Tilly stops her work and stands up abruptly.

"Walk with me then."

Tilly takes Camas by the hand, walks to the elder's Moroccan tent, and pulls a cord on a bell outside the door flap. Max comes to the door and welcomes them in.

"You're still here," Camas says to Max.

"Yes. Quite a bit left to get to *no trace*."

"Here's a gift," Camas says flirtatiously and gives him a boob necklace.

"Wow, thank you," Max says appreciatively. He gives them both a hug. "How was the wedding?"

"It didn't happen," Tilly says, trying to keep her chin up to hold back the tears.

Max holds her hands, "I hold a space of love for you and what is meant to be."

"Thank you." She hugs him again. "Can we talk?" Tilly asks.

Max leads them to a carpet with poufs in a circle. He pulls three of them together, facing each other. They sit.

"What is it, brave one?"

"I got a call from a woman in Napa."

"You didn't tell me she's in the wine country. Why couldn't we have gone there for your bachelorette par...?" Stops herself, sorry for bringing up the wedding.

"She wants to get rid of cars in her town," Tilly continues.

"That won't happen," Camas says.

"Not all of the cars but to turn the town into a bike town."

"That's a big undertaking," Max says.

"Utrecht did it."

"You tech, what?" Camas asks.

"Utrecht. It's a city in the Netherlands. Like Napa, parents were fed up with kids getting hit and killed on their bikes so they created bike-only roads. A lot of them."

"People are lazy and will still drive."

"They also made the bike roads faster and more direct, so

39

in many cases, it's faster and more convenient to be on a bike."

"That sounds like an important project," Max adds.

"I think so too."

"Great, thanks for sharing it with me." Max stands up. "I wish you both a safe trip home."

Tilly remains seated. "There's something else."

"Uh, oh. I knew there was something else. I see the look in your eyes," Camas says.

Max sits back down. Samprati walks in. Max motions to her to join them.

Tilly sits up very straight and looks straight at Camas. "You know, I think it's time we played with the big girls."

"What does that mean?" Camas asks.

"The house is on fire."

"Greta Thundberg's quote," Samprati says.

"Yes. So, if your house is on fire, you can't just take one town and convert it to bikes."

Camas looks serious, trying to understand. "Huh?" She finally realizes Tilly's meaning. "Oh, no. No way."

"Camas, it's the only way."

CHAPTER 14

RISER BAR: A TYPE OF HANDLEBAR WITH A U SHAPE IN THE MIDDLE

L iam opens the door to Tilly's cottage, where they have been living together. He brings his very dusty suitcase in, sets it by the front door, and unzips it. He goes into the bedroom, opens a drawer, takes out some clothes, and puts them into the suitcase. He feels the ring box in his pocket. He opens it, looks at the two wedding bands, then puts it back and pulls out an envelope. He sets it down on a side table in front of a framed photo of Tilly, Pedro and him at Sandglass city beach.

Liam dives off of Graeme's dock into the lake. He swims strongly.

"When you say every city, do you mean every city in the world?" Max asks.

"Not exactly, I mean every city and every town in the world," Tilly responds.

"Well, you are certainly talking to someone who likes grand plans," Samprati says.

"I know! You just pulled off such a huge feat. That's why I'm here to ask you to help us." She turns to Camas, "And to ask you to help me too."

"Do what?" Camas asks.

"Did you know that the bicycle was instrumental in women achieving the right to vote?"

"Nope," Camas answers.

"It was. It provided them the freedom of movement to enhance their lives overall but also to spread the word of the suffrage movement."

"What does that have to do with Napa becoming a bike town?"

"I want you and I to ride across the country with a bike manifesto."

"Ride what?"

"And the manifesto will include practical plans for towns and cities to make the change. We'll personally deliver it and explain it."

"We might have some resources in our coffers that could help with some media outreach," Max says.

"I was hoping, with the help of the city leaders of Utrecht, the elders of Burning Man would develop the plans. They've done it. You've done it."

He looks at Samprati with a serious look. She smiles.

"We will need to get consensus from the others, but I believe that, if you can get Utrecht onboard, we'll join as well," Max says.

"Well, I guess I know what I'm doing for spring break," Camas says, laughing. "Following my crazy best friend across the continent. You still didn't explain the suffragette part."

"Remember what Rock said about shareholders deciding whether to buy or sell oil shares? We'll be asking them to cast their vote for the bike."

Samprati walks over to a desk and comes back with a newspaper. "When Max was helping us make a decision not to allow cars in Black Rock City, I did some research on my own, and I found this old newspaper, The San Francisco Call. Back in 1895, it said, 'It really doesn't matter much where this one individual young lady is going on her wheel. It may be that she's going to the park on pleasure bent, or to the store for a dozen hairpins, or to call on a sick friend at the other side of town, or a recipe for removing tan and freckles. Let that be as it may. What the interested public wishes to know is, where are all the women on wheels going? Is there a grand rendezvous somewhere toward which they are all headed and where they will some time hold a meet that will cause this wobbly old world to wake up and readjust itself?'"

Camas reaches out and grabs Tilly's hand.

CHAPTER 15

BICYCLE BELL: A PERCUSSIVE SIGNALING INSTRUMENT MOUNTED ON A BICYCLE FOR WARNING PEDESTRIANS AND OTHER CYCLISTS USUALLY THUMB-ACTIVATED

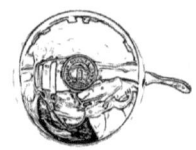

Goosey and her father, Sherman, Goosey's assistant, another Butimines employee, and the corporate attorney sit around a large conference table. They each have laptops, and Goosey's computer is set up with a free-standing microphone and high-tech camera. Her assistant is hovering to make sure everything works well.

"Welcome to the third quarter shareholder update, ladies and gentlemen." Goosey rudely waves off her assistant. Her assistant sits down.

"We are pleased to report strong results. Revenue from the…"

Ana sits at a grand piano in the living room of a 1920's Spanish Hollywood-era bungalow with elegant period furnishings wearing a sexy slim-fitting satin 1950's dress. She plays a melancholy classical piece. She stops playing and walks to the picture window, which overlooks Los Angeles from the hillside. Thick smog covers the city, and the skyscrapers of downtown and the iconic Hollywood sign are barely visible through the pollution.

She taps her phone.

"Darling, how can I be happy breathing this dreadful air? I could see from Santa Barbara to Mexico in my past life," she says with an elegant old Hollywood lilt.

She listens.

"Thank you. No, I don't know how you'll fix it."

She listens.

"Thank you for trying. Love you, dear one."

CHAPTER 16

CRANK ARMS: THE PEDALS SCREW INTO THE CRANK ARMS WHICH BOLT ONTO THE BOTTOM BRACKET SPINDLE

Graeme answers his phone at the wheel of Liz's 1971 Volkswagen van.

"Tilly."

"Hi."

"Are you OK?"

"I miss him."

"I'm sure you do. He misses you too. He's been swimming a lot and helping make some repairs on my old cottage."

The line is silent.

"Are you still there?" Graeme asks.

"I'm calling to see if you can set up a time for us to have a video meeting with the mayor of Utrecht when you get there."

"Liz and I are headed to the airport."

"Hi, Tilly," Liz calls out from the passenger seat.

"I'll get that set up and let you know." Graeme pauses. "Tilly, as self-centered as this may sound because I would love nothing more than to have you as my daughter-in-law, sometimes there are things in our past that hold us back from what we want and deserve."

"Travel safely," Tilly says quietly.

Tilly sits on the steps of her porch and texts Camas, *Meet me at Heaven's Brothers tomorrow at 8:00 am.*

Camas texts back, *Damn girl, that's too early.*

Set your alarm.

Duh. Love you.

Tilly calls Ella.

"Tilly! Great to hear from you. Congratulations on your wedding."

Tilly looks down, looks around as if people could hear her. "Oh, thanks. How is everything going?" she says weakly.

"We've rallied more support in the community by contacting other schools, and the Napa tourism board and winery associations feel the plan will help bring more visitors to the valley. We've got a meeting with the chamber of commerce on Tuesday. I'm sure they'll have lots of questions we can't answer, but at least we'll know their questions."

"That's great!"

"Can you be on a call with me and some others at 8:00 am?"

"Sure. Tilly, thank you so much for helping our little town."

"I overheard a guy say to his friend, 'you know they say that we drive a car and ride a bike, but it's actually the other way around. You ride a car and drive a bike.'"

"I never thought of that. It's so true!"

"Nice call this morning," Rock says as he walks along White Rock Lake near the Dallas Arboretum, his southern drawl dripping over the phone line.

"Well, thank you. Rock. You're always so charming. When are you going to invite me to dinner?" Goosey asks flirtatiously.

"Um," he stammers. "I'm sure that would be nice," he says unconvincingly.

"Yes, I'm sure it would be too," Goosey purrs.

"Listen, Goosey, I've already spoken with your father a bit about this and wanted to bring you into the loop."

"Yes?"

"My investment company is launching a new tool that will issue a performance rating based on sustainability and renewable energy. We've hired Gold Knights to process the data and help us with the user interface."

"Sounds fancy."

"It will provide a color-coded value of an energy company's sustainable practices, green being good, yellow being *we're trying*, red being coal and fracking."

"Aww, Rock. Why'd ya have to go out and do a crazy thing like that? Aren't you almost in retirement?"

"Let's just say I was inspired."

"Well, I look marvelous in a red dress."

"Well, I guess it remains to be seen if your shareholders hold on to you in your red dress."

"I just want you to hold on to me."

CHAPTER 17

DERAILER: A DEVICE THAT IS BOLTED TO THE FRAME THAT HANDLES THE JOB OF MOVING THE CHAIN FROM ONE GEAR TO ANOTHER WHEN GEARS ARE SHIFTED

H undreds upon hundreds of bicycles ride through the city of Utrecht. The people on two wheels are going to work, buying groceries, toting kids, hauling cargo deliveries, having romantic picnics, and breathing fresh air. The bikes move quickly and efficiently. There is a logjam of car traffic on an adjacent street, a drastic contrast to the smooth flowing bike riders.

Graeme and Liz ride a bike through the city. They hear the upbeat song *The Times Are Changing* by Graeme James playing when they are stopped at a light in front of a sidewalk café. They park in a high tech bike parking structure and walk to the Utrecht City Hall.

The elevator opens, and they receive a warm welcome from Mayor Bram Van Zaken, mayor of Utrecht, who has short grey hair, is in his sixties and wears a sports jacket over a white shirt, no tie. He is joined by Fenna Weil, Director of Transportation, wearing bike shorts with a shorter skirt over them and a Utrecht bicycle-logoed polo shirt, and Luuk

Couperus, Director of Cultural Affairs, who has dirty blonde hair in a man bun and wears a fashionable shirt, trim pants with colorful socks and sky-blue loafers. They shake hands with Graeme and Liz, lead them to the conference room and connect to the meeting on a large computer screen hanging on the wall.

Tilly and Camas sit with Mayor Patrick, mayor of Sandglass, who is in his thirties, handsome, in jeans and a button-down shirt, at a table at Heaven's Brothers café. Max sits at a handmade wood conference table with Samprati, Sharu, Shasta, and Plume in a building with a view of the San Francisco skyline. Ella is with Mayor Dandy and looks surprised by all of the faces in the meeting.

"Thanks for coming, everyone," Tilly says to the group.

The group smiles and nods.

"Ella von Walzer, is the one who asked me to help her town of Napa become a bike town. Ella, your project has grown in scope. We've asked the city leaders in Utrecht to help us. Mayor Bran Van Zaken, Fenna, director of transportation, and Luuk, director of cultural affairs, are here with us today. Graeme and Liz traveled from Sandglass to be with them. Also here on the call are the elders of Burning Man who just converted their Black Rock City from cars to bikes this year. Max, Samprati, Sharu, Shasta, and Plume. Patrick, the mayor of our town of Sandglass, is sitting here with me along with Camas, who is CFO of One More Year. Welcome, all!"

Everyone shares greetings of "hello," "welcome," "hallo."

"Tilly, why don't you give everyone an overview," Graeme says.

"Sure. I've asked Camas to cycle across the United States with me with the goal of a nation-wide "car out" when we reach Washington DC and a commitment from half of the towns and cities when we arrive that they will implement an ongoing bike first plan."

Ella gasps. "Wow, that is an expansion of the scope!"

"Sure is," Camas responds.

"I know it seems huge, but here's how I think we can pull it off. Can you all hear me OK?" Tilly asks.

"Yes, go ahead," Graeme encourages.

"First, we will create a manifesto. The..."

"I think we need a catchy name for it," Camas interrupts Tilly.

Tilly smiles. "The manifesto will go out by mail and social media to all towns and cities. This is why we need your help, to create an easy to follow plan 'how to to become a bike first city.' It will come in three sizes: city, small city, and town."

"You know, there are 929 CBSA's, statistical areas 10,000 population plus. Then you have the small towns. 31,000 of them. That's a huge undertaking," Sharu says.

"Yes, but it *is* a finite number. That's positive," Tilly says enthusiastically.

The Utrecht group looks at one another. The Burning Man group looks at one another. Then they break into broad smiles because of Tilly's unbridled optimism.

"Go on, please, Tilly," Max says.

"Utrecht has already implemented the plan for a city, and they are also creating a brand new bike-only city from scratch. Bravo, by the way."

"Thank you," Bram, Fenna, and Luuk say in unison.

"They'll be instrumental in the city part of the manifesto, and oversee the other sized plans, if you agree. We're also proposing that Ella and Mayor Dandy create the small city plan, and Mayor Patrick the town plan. All of the plans will have the same core elements and mission statement of the manifesto but tailored for implementation," Tilly explains.

"Sounds like you want people to actually use it," Mayor Bram says.

"Exactly!"

Camas continues, "Tilly and I will launch our bike ride on March 1st from the west coast of Washington state. That gives us about four and a half months to prepare the manifesto and get the word out."

"Max has agreed to lead the logistics of the ride," Tilly says.

"I think we could get some worldwide participation too," Bram says.

"That would be great!"

"You know that big oil and the auto industry are not going to sit idly by, don't you," Sharu warns. "People believe being American is the freedom to get into their gas guzzler and drive across the country."

"That will need to be addressed as part of the public relations message," Liz offers.

"We're not trying to stop people from seeing the country. Well, maybe just a little — some parts of nature need to live in peace. Our goal is to show people that living their everyday life on a bike is better than in a car."

"Millennials are living that way already. They don't own a car, and then they'll use a car-share service to go camping or out of town," Samprati says.

"If you staged your ride with some two-day stops, we could add some live music and try to get some well-known artists to lend their name to the cause," Plume suggests.

"Yes, we'll be stopping to meet with city leaders to discuss the manifesto."

"Great."

"What's the route, and how long will it take you," mayor Patrick asks.

"Here's a map," Tilly says, sharing her screen. "We're

going to ride the Great American Rail Trail, which is 3,700 miles. If we ride 60 miles a day..."

"Ouch," Camas says.

"...and allowing ourselves some days for meetings, we should arrive in DC the first week in June. Camas thinks we need some type of gifts for the towns."

"Hell yeah. It's harder to shoot at somebody bringing you a present."

"You think you'll be shot at?" Fenna asks, shocked.

"Camas exaggerates, but it is true that there are some very staid, conservative people, who aren't going to understand it," Graeme explains.

"What if the gifts were tulip bulbs?" Luuk ask. "That would be a fine connection to Utrecht and the Netherlands."

"The cost aside, that's a logistical challenge," Max says.

"I have some favors to call in with some tulip producers. I think we could get them at a very reasonable cost, but I can see the issue of traveling on bikes with millions of bulbs," Mayor Bram says.

"We could mail them out with the manifesto," Plume suggests. "A trojan horse if you will. Tie in some kind of PR as you ride in. Path of petals. Something like that."

"I like it," Tilly smiles. "Ella and Mayor Dandy, what do you think?"

"It sounds verdomd geweldig," Ella says.

Bram, Fenna and Luke laugh.

"What's that?" Graeme asks.

"*Fucking awesome* in Dutch," Luuk says, smiling.

Ella continues, "We are actually going to turn this town into a livable, healthier, safer place."

"Mayor Patrick? Thoughts?"

"I can't guarantee the conservative elements in town will support it, but if anyone could convince them, it's you, Tilly."

"OK, we're a go!" Max takes control. "How's this for the

task force? Tilly and Camas, you are our front line poster children and master communicators of the manifesto."

Camas puts her arm around Tilly proudly.

"Plume and Luuk, can you two work together on the communication plan?"

"Yes." Plume gives Luuk the thumbs up. Luuk reciprocates.

"Mayor Bram, can you work with Samprati and Sharu to develop the universal list of towns and cities and their mayor contacts?"

"It would be my honor," Bram says.

"Ours as well, Mayor." Samprati smiles.

"Shasta will work with me on the ride logistics."

"Yes, sir!"

"Fenna, will you work with Mayor Patrick and Mayor Dandy to develop their bike first plans, and Pat and Dandy, will you document the details for the town and small city bike first plans?"

"Sounds great," Fenna says.

"Thanks, Fenna," Mayor Patrick says.

"Yes, we truly appreciate your commitment to bicycles and your experience," Mayor Dandy adds.

"Ella, as you gather support in your town, will you document the steps and organizations that you enlist for support so we can use that in plans?"

"Will do!"

"One other task, Mayor Bram, could you work with Graeme and Liz to solidify the large city version of the plan? Hopefully, since you've already created your city, it won't be too onerous."

"It won't be a problem at all. Graeme and Liz, thank you for visiting us."

"Thank you!" Graeme and Liz say warmly.

Max gets louder, "To make this come together, we need to

have the manifesto mailing out by New Year's Day. Three month's away. Is everyone on board with this timing?"

Graeme, Liz and the Utrecht group nod at each other.

"Utrecht on board," Graeme says.

"We're in," Mayor Dandy says as Ella nods enthusiastically.

"I'll get it done," Patrick says.

"I see challenges, but we're behind you, man," Sharu says. Max walks around his table and shakes all of their hands and embraces them.

"You're stuck with us," Camas says.

The group laughs.

"What if we call it Petal Pedal Ride," Shasta suggests.

"Is that Petal Pedal or Pedal Petal?" Tilly asks.

"I think either works," Plume says.

"It's a little girlie," Camas says, scrunching her face.

"I'm girlie. What's wrong with girlie?" tattooed Shasta says gruffly wearing her ballcap turned backward, T-shirt and leather jacket covered with bike club patches.

"And we are girls," Tilly says.

"True."

"Women power! Tulip flower power. *The Great Petal Pedal Ride* it is!"

CHAPTER 18

SADDLE WRENCH: A TOOL FOR TIGHTENING THE SADDLE ON SOME, USUALLY VINTAGE, BICYCLES

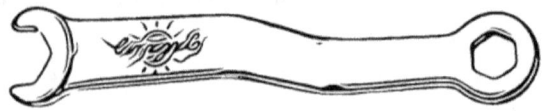

Liam's strong arm muscles glisten with sweat as he hammers vigorously on the roofline of Graeme's quaint cottage on Opal Island. He stands above lilac bushes on a ladder wearing jeans and no shirt. He misses the nail and hits his finger with the hammer.

"Damn it!"

He puts the finger into his mouth and continues the work. He answers his phone.

"Hey, Dad."

Graeme is sitting at an outdoor table at a Utrecht café with Liz, bikes whizzing by. "How are things going?"

"They suck, actually."

"Go see her, Liam."

"She called to tell me she got my letter and that she misses me. I told her I needed some more time."

"Time for what?"

"I'm just busy, that's all. I'm training and working on the cottage."

"She'll be leaving soon for a few months."

"She told me."

"Don't wait too long."

Liam looks over to the tandem bike Graeme had given them at Burning Man. He resumes hammering forcefully.

CHAPTER 19
FRAME: THE MAIN STRUCTURAL PART OF THE BICYCLE, COMMONLY MADE OF STEEL, ALUMINUM, TITANIUM, OR CARBON FIBER

"I can't believe they assigned us the hardest part," Camas says, sitting with Tilly at Heaven's Brothers. Camas looks at her Macbook. Tilly has a notebook and pen.

"I'm pretty sure we assigned it to ourselves, but everyone else has hard parts too. The details of a city bike plan, for example."

"True, but this is the part that may make the whole thing work... or not."

"What do you mean?"

"A manifesto is the inspirational vision."

"You surprise me sometimes," Tilly smiles.

"How's that?"

"You pretend not to care, and then you always seem to get to the heart of the matter."

"I am heart, sista."

"Yes, you are."

"What have you got so far?"

Tilly reads from her notebook, "We ride a bicycle to save the planet."

"That's too tame."

"Aww," a little hurt. "I guess you're right. Tame is better than lame, I guess."

"It's a little lame too," Camas teases, then turns serious. "It's got to be strong enough to grab people. Stronger than this double espresso." She picks up her phone, "I found some things online. There's even a manifesto handbook."

"Like what?" Tilly asks.

"We'll need a list of tenets, of course. Those will be in the plans coming from the mayors, but it also needs an intro, a preamble, that's short with a sense of urgency."

"Did you just use the word preamble?" Tilly smiles.

"It also says it needs some theater," Camas says.

Tilly and Camas sit working at a picnic table at Sylvester Bay park overlooking Lake Bijou Nez.

"I think our tulips and the fact we're riding across the country covers that."

"I think it needs to be in writing, too," Camas responds.

"OK."

"It also needs to challenge and provoke," Camas says, reading from her laptop.

"Hmmm..." Tilly says, thinking, looking out over the lake.

Camas types into her laptop and Tilly writes some things down in her notebook.

Many people ride up in front of Camas and Tilly's outdoor table at Heaven's Brothers and put their bikes into the nearly-full bike rack.

A couple comes out of the café, unlocks their bikes, have a sweet romantic kiss, and ride in two separate directions.

"And it needs to be magic," Tilly says dreamily.

CHAPTER 20

WINE BOTTLE CARRIER: A BRILLIANT BICYCLE ACCESSORY TO CARRY A BOTTLE OF WINE TO A PICNIC OR OTHER FESTIVE DESTINATION

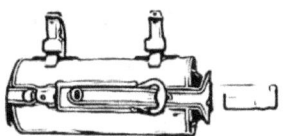

The days and weeks that follow see a *manifesto montage* of bikes, bulbs, and early brouhaha as preparations for The Great Petal Pedal Ride are underway.

Tilly and Camas choose a bike for the ride at Reeve's bike shop in Sandglass. Reeve, late forties, fit, salt and pepper hair, also referred to as one of the Sandglass Bike Guys, gets them set up. A *previously owned* sign hangs over the bikes they choose. They laugh joyfully and wave at friends on the patio of MatchLove Brewery as they take a ride around the block.

Graeme, Liz and Bram tour Utrecht on bikes. Bram stops to point out various features of the design of the bike-only streets for the city plan.

Ella is in her garage with tall stacks of girl scout cookies. She talks about the bike first plan as the girls and moms come to pick up the cookies. She hands them each a bike first flyer.

Shasta and Max put colored pins and a string along the bike route on a massive map of the U.S. on the wall of the Burning Man conference room. They mark radiuses around the metro areas on the trail. Samprati sits in front of a large screen marking the route on a GIS map.

Tulip bulbs in large harvest crates at a tulip farm outside of Utrecht are loaded into a shipping container, then onto a truck, then onto a ship.

Liam puts the tandem bike into Graeme's wood boat and heads to Sandglass.

Rock is at a grassy park near the lake in Dallas following his two-year-old grandson on a no-pedals European-style toddler bike. The boy pushes himself along joyously.

Mayor Patrick stands in front of a Town Hall meeting in Sandglass. He shows a map of bike paths through the city, green for existing paths, yellow for proposed. An area shaded in purple with a walking icon denotes a pedestrian-only section of downtown.

Mayor Dandy rides his bike through the vineyards on the Vine Trail. He has wine hanging from the center bar and a *Re-elect Mayor Dandy* sign on the rear. He stops to talk with people picnicking in the vineyards with their bikes and hands them a bike first flyer.

Ella talks on her phone in a large parking lot as her daughter and the girl scouts get their bikes adjusted and safety training from the local bike club.

Mayor Patrick walks with Sandgass city planners holding a large stencil of a bike path symbol.

Ella shows the bike map plan in front of people seated at rows of tables at a formal wine tasting. Many smile and nod their heads.

Plume and Luuk sit at their computers with a drawing of a tulip basket planned for the front of Tilly and Camas's bikes.

With large maps and diagrams on each of their office walls, Graeme and Bram in Utrecht, Mayor Patrick and Tilly in Sandglass, and Mayor Dandy and Ella in Napa, make edits, draw graphics, and video conference with each other, to refine the town and city bike first plans.

Camas and Tilly sit at Heaven's Brothers and read the first press about the ride. *Triathlete Tilly DeMontagne will ride across the country to champion the bicycle.*

Manifesto booklets and city plans are packed in boxes with tulip bulbs with instructions: *1) Read the Manifesto, 2) Plant the tulips as a sign of your support, and 3) Brag it up online and tag #petalpedalride.*

Liam rides by Tilly's cottage on the tandem bike. He turns around, passes by again, slows down, then rides on.

Manifesto-tulip packages are carried by diligent mail carriers across the country in every weather condition into small, medium, and large city hall buildings in styles from Modern to Art Deco to Neoclassical to Beaux-Arts to Italianate to Greek Revival to Federal.

CHAPTER 21

MAP CASE: WATERPROOF CASE TO VIEW A PRINT MAP ON THE HANDLEBARS

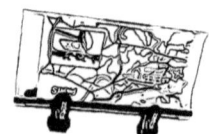

Tilly, Camas, Max, Shasta, and Plume sit in a gondola over the magical, dramatic Spokane River Falls.

"Here's the itinerary. It has the route and where you'll camp each night. Study it at least through the first week," Max says, handing Camas and Tilly each a paper.

Tilly nods. "Thanks for delivering it in person."

"You're welcome. It's in your email too, of course, but I had to see this Inland Northwest you talk so much about. Pretty spectacular!"

"And why are we camping again?" Camas asks.

"Because we're not fancy."

"You're not fancy. I, on the other hand, am quite fancy."

"Some places will be remote. And it's more like glamping. You'll have air mattresses, good food." Max answers.

"OK, then. What's the buzz?" Camas asks Plume.

"Just a small but significant hum from the manifestos and tulip bulbs landing. We plan to send out our marketing push once you leave La Push, so we should have some genuine interest by the time you reach Seattle," Plume answers.

"We could send the manifesto-tulip packages to the major newspapers," Camas suggests.

"Look at you, Ms. Public Relations," Tilly teases.

"Great idea, Camas. Yes, we thought of that, and they'll land right as you're starting the ride."

"How are you two feeling? Ready?" Max asks.

"I feel like I'd rather spend two months on the beach, actually," Camas says. She looks at Tilly, "but I committed."

"Just think what great legs you'll have by the end," Tilly says.

"Josh is excited about that." Camas looks down at her legs.

They laugh.

"I have a practice session with Mayor Patrick to present the manifesto as though he's a mayor on the road."

"Good idea. I'm going to run the ride from San Francisco, and Shasta will be in your support van along with Plume. We'll rotate some helpers in and out along the route. Once we get a few more supplies in Seattle, we've got everything you asked for, including Camas's beer."

"Damn right. If I'm going to be riding 60 miles a day for 3,700 miles, I need an ice-cold beer at the end of the day. Max, you're the man!"

Camas gives him a high five as the group exits the gondola.

"Yes, you are." Tilly hugs Max and holds on.

"You ride like the wind and sing your song to all who will listen," Max says as they hug.

"I will."

CHAPTER 22

PADDLEBOARD TRAILER: A TWO-WHEEL CARRIER TO TRANSPORT A KAYAK OR STAND-UP PADDLEBOARD

Tilly rows across the lake to Graeme's island on her paddleboard. Roxie greets her excitedly at the dock. She looks and sniffs around for Pedro.

"Sorry, Roxie. P's still sailing the world."

Roxie whimpers. Tilly ties her board to the dock, then runs up the trail. She arrives, breathing heavily, at the top. Liam stands on a ladder painting trim on the cottage. He is startled to see her and smiles weakly.

"You're winded. That's a rare sight," he says gently.

"No kidding. Too much paper and computers. Not enough mountains."

Liam gets off the ladder. They embrace.

"How's it all going? Dad fills me in a little bit."

Tilly smiles.

"Well, he fills me in a lot. I miss you."

Tilly holds his hands as they stand face-to-face. Roxie tries to edge her way between them for attention with the beautiful Lake Bijou Nez behind them.

"I miss you too."

"You miss me so much you're riding a bike to the opposite side of the country?" Liam asks, searching.

Tilly keeps a hold of his hands but doesn't answer. Liam lets go of her hands and turns to face the lake.

Tilly rests a hand and her cheek on the back of his shoulder and closes her eyes.

CHAPTER 23

HEX WRENCH SET: TOOLS, ALSO KNOWN AS ALLEN WRENCHES, TO TURN HEX BOLTS WHICH HOLD TOGETHER NEARLY EVERY COMPONENT ON A MODERN BIKE

Huge waves crash onto La Push Beach, where Shasta and Plume sit inside a parked 1994 Econoline E-1501 Van with a trailer carrying a rack of bikes and containers of supplies. Inside the van are high-tech screens for their communication with Max and Plume's monitoring of marketing efforts. There are well-organized and beautiful bike tools on a section of a wall.

Camas knocks on the driver side window.

"Hey, ladies, ya ready?" Shasta asks as she opens the van door. Shasta wears long camouflage shorts, a leather belt, a red tank top, and Doc Marten boots.

"Let's do it!" Camas responds.

"We want to show you some things before you start tomorrow," Shasta says. She pulls bikes off of the trailer and rolls them to Tilly and Camas.

"We've added a few things since you've been on your bikes. You both have three Go Pros. One on your helmet, one on the front of your bike, and one on the back. You don't have to worry about them, other than knowing that Luuk and I will be piecing together footage for promotions. Max will also be using it to keep an eye on you as well."

"Good to know. No outside naked showers, Big Brother," Camas jokes.

"If you were to have a big brother, he's the one you'd want," Shasta says without smiling.

Camas looks at Tilly and says under her breath, "She's miss personality."

"Here are your hydration packs, and your bikes have a spot for your energy bars, donated by Bluff Bar, here," Shasta continues.

"Cama..." Tilly starts.

"They paid for five One More Year billboards, so I agreed that we'd bring them. No obligation to eat it in front of the camera or anything."

Tilly looks relieved.

"Here are GPS watches for both of you. We want you to turn them on for all of your riding. You know how to use those from your racing, I assume."

"Yup," Camas answers.

"We'll use those to get stats on the distance and time and also to do some social media with cycling groups. The satellite will also let the dot watchers live track you," Plume, wearing a long flowing tie-dye dress with a matching headband, adds.

"These watches can dive to 50 meters, signal to us and emergency responders if you need help, and take photos," Shasta says.

"Wow, I feel like James Bond being given his spy gadgets by Algy," Camas says, impressed.

Tilly and Plume smile. Shasta is serious. She calls Max from Tilly's watch.

"Hey girls, nice to see you," Max says, his face on the watch screen.

"Hi, Max. I appreciate all of the forethought in the bike additions. I like things used and simple. I don't need these fancy things."

"We want you to be safe, and we want to be able to stay in touch," Max says.

"We also added something fun," Plume says as she pulls two pots filled with colorful tulips and places them in a holder on the front of the bikes.

Tilly and Camas smile.

"Pretty!" Tilly says.

"It is, but won't that be heavy for us to carry the whole way?" Camas asks.

"Yes, and impractical," Shasta adds disapprovingly.

"Luuk and I wanted something to tie into the tulip bulb gifts. They aren't heavy. We found an artist in Seattle who makes them from silk. Feel it," she instructs.

Tilly and Camas pick them up. "Yeah, it is light," Camas says. "Hey, what's this light on the pot?"

Plume taps Camas's new smartwatch and upbeat dance music starts playing. Camas and Tilly laugh and start dancing.

"See, not completely impractical!" Plume says to Shasta, smiling.

"Cool! I was going to ask about tunes!"

"Nice van by the way," Max admires.

"Tilly made us get the '94. We wanted the new model but it's pretty cool," Shasta says.

"It's the year you were born," Camas says.

Tilly smiles.

"Keep your stuff longer, people, right? Looks like you're all set," Max says. "We'll leave at six hundred hours tomorrow. Get good rest."

CHAPTER 24

BAR ENDS: THE ANGLED EXTENSIONS ATTACHED TO THE ENDS OF SOME FLAT HANDLEBARS AND RISER HANDLEBARS THAT PROVIDE AN ALTERNATE PLACE TO REST HANDS

Ana sips vermouth in a martini glass in 1960's Laura Petri-style pencil pants, flats, a short sleeve cashmere sweater with pearls, and a colorful silk headband. The sun is getting low, and the warm light creates a glow on the Art Deco bungalow furnishings. She refills her drink and sits on a velvet chaise and opens a newspaper. She notices the article about the Great Petal Pedal Ride, reaches over languidly to pet a white long-haired cat, then picks up her phone.

"Darling, can you please drive me to Chicago?" Ana says in a regal, elegant voice.

"You have the show at the Bowl next week," Topper reminds her.

"We'll leave after that then."

"Alright."

"Oh, by the way, we'll be using the carriage from the Exotica show. It's bigger than the rickshaw."

"The e-bike carriage?"

"Yes, darling. Remember your days making money with that bicycle carriage before you became a big star?"

"I remember."

"There's a movement afoot that needs a bit more drama and momentum."

"That's the old Route 66, you know."

"How marvelous! I'll tell my devoted fans. You hire whomever you need to help us with the journey. At least one cargo bike for my costumes, please."

"I knew things would never be dull with you. I'd carry you to the ends of the earth, my love."

"Thank you, dear one. Ciao."

CHAPTER 25

BASKET: A CONTAINER FOR CARRYING CARGO, OFTEN MOUNTED ON THE HANDLEBARS AND MADE OF TRADITIONAL BASKET WEAVING MATERIALS SUCH AS WICKER AND CANE

Tilly talks on her cell phone as Camas sits in front of a campfire with two tents behind her on the beach. Waves crash onto tall rock formations near the shore.

"Liam?" Camas asks as Tilly walks back.

"Yeah," Tilly says softly. "He wishes us a safe ride."

"That's nice." Camas looks out to the ocean. "I'm a little nervous."

"It's not too late to bow out."

"Do you want Liam to come instead?"

"Of course not."

"Just promise me we'll stick together on this journey."

"Which journey are we talking about, just to be clear."

"Any and all."

"OK." Tilly puts her head on Camas's shoulder.

Ana and Topper perform at the Hollywood Bowl in a punk rock cabaret show. Ana is luxuriously stylish in a 1930's evening gown, white geisha-girl face paint with dramatic painted eyebrows and bright red lips. Topper wears his signature glitter hotpant-shorts, a top hat, and platform boots. A theatrical hardcore rock song mentions bikes and suffragettes.

Camas is excited as they prepare to get on their bikes to depart. She wears fuchsia-colored bike shorts, brightly patterned knee-high cycling socks, and a Great Petal Pedal Ride T-shirt with a long sleeve cycling jersey underneath. She waves to people in the campground. They give her a strange who-are-you look.

Shasta drives up in the van and loads the tents. "We'll see you in Port Townsend."

Plume gets out of the passenger side with her camera. Tilly, wearing earth-tone mountain bike shorts and an *OMY - One More Year* jersey, and Camas stand over their bikes with their arms around each other's shoulders.

"This is it. Mile zero," Tilly says, looking toward the highway.

"No sweat. Let's do this, sista!"

Camas takes off energetically. She rides in front of Tilly and waves to all of the passing cars. Tilly smiles at her enthusiasm and waves occasionally too. After fifteen miles, Camas musters a smile with just a few waves. After thirty miles, Camas doesn't smile but waves to an occasional car. By forty miles, Camas is grumpy and already tired.

Camas and Tilly take a rest stop at a tiny Washington town.

"Where are the fans? What kind of PR job is Plume and that prancing Dutchman doing anyway?"

"We're not really here for the fans."

"The hell we're not," Camas says as she reluctantly gets back on her bike to resume the ride.

Camas trudges very slowly up the stairs to the top deck of the Bainbridge Island Ferry with her helmet on, exhausted from the first stretch of the ride. They walk to the bow and see the Seattle skyline in the distance.

"That was fucking hard."

"But pretty."

"Pretty fucking hard. All the riding and those mountains near the coast and the mayor of Port Angeles wouldn't even meet with us."

"He probably already had appointments."

"Uh-huh," Camas says skeptically.

CHAPTER 26

FREEHUB BODY: TRANSFERS POWER TO YOUR WHEEL WHEN PEDALING FORWARD, BUT ALLOWS THE REAR WHEEL TO TURN FREELY WHEN PEDALING BACKWARDS OR NOT PEDALING AT ALL

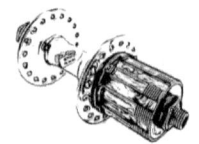

C amas and Tilly ride their bikes off of the ferry. A group of twelve diverse people on bikes in street clothes, wild-looking bike messenger garb, and road bike lycra are waiting for them.

"Some fans for you!" Tilly jokes.

Camas gives them a wave and smiles. They follow Camas and Tilly through Seattle, past the Space Needle to Seattle Center, to La Marzocco Café, the home of KEXP Radio Station.

"The mayor is meeting you at the café," Shasta tells Tilly on her watch phone.

"Got it. Thanks."

They lock their bikes and shake hands with the people who rode with them.

The Seattle mayor, a petite Asian woman in her mid-fifties, stands as she sees Tilly and Camas enter. They walk to her table and greet her. They shake hands with the mayor and the Seattle Deputy Mayor, a tall, lanky man in his thirties with a ponytail.

"Thanks for meeting with us," Tilly says.

"Bram Van Zaken called me and said I should say yes."

"Can I get you a coffee?" Camas asks.

"I'm all set, thank you," the mayor responds.

"I'll take a double espresso," the deputy mayor requests.

Camas nods. "I'll get the coffee. You go ahead." Camas smiles and talks with people in line. The KEXP *On Air* light is illuminated across the room.

Tilly presents the Petal Pedal manifesto and large city bike first plan to the mayor. She pages through the material, pointing out key items. Camas returns with coffee.

"We have some of this in place, but I can see that the manifesto is asking us to fully commit to bicycles."

"Yes, that's right."

"I'll review this with my staff and get some community feedback.

"Did you plant the tulips?" Camas asks.

"Not yet."

"As a gesture of support, maybe you can start with that?" Camas suggests.

"I think I can make that happen."

"When?" Camas asks pointedly.

Tilly gives Camas a look. The mayor looks at her deputy mayor.

"We could plant them at the park bandshell, next to the city bike path," he offers.

The mayor turns back to Tilly and Camas, "Next week?"

Graeme and Liz bicycle on the coast of Madeira Island. They stop on a hill and see sailboats in the distance, then ride down into the village marina to greet Moore, Spit, Anika, and Pedro as Moore's sailboat is pulling up to the dock. Moore steers the boat carefully. Spit is very excited to be near shore. Both young men have grown beards on their trip across the Atlantic. Anika is elegant in a bikini top and short sarong. She helps Moore prepare to tie up, lowering buoys, moving ropes.

"Ahoy there!" Spit yells, waving wildly.

"Greetings, sailors!" Liz calls back.

Anika throws Graeme a rope, and Graeme ties them to the dock. They hug with much laughter and some tears of happiness. Pedro jumps and barks in excitement.

"Done. Let's get a beer," Camas says walking towards the door of the café. Plume rushes up.

"KEXP wants to give you some air time," Plume says excitedly.

"We're not musicians," Tilly says.

"I play the bongos," Camas says.

Tilly laughs.

"They heard about your cause and want to meet you since you're here."

Tilly and Camas wear headsets sitting across from the DJ, indie alternative music playing in the background.

"Will you share from your Great Petal Pedal Ride manifesto?"

The music continues below Tilly's strong voice.

"I feel the power of my legs to carry me on this bicycle to smell the fresh air, to buy a sweet, crisp apple that fell from a tree a few miles from here, and to sit a spell with you."

The music matches the rhythm of a boombox at Santa Monica Pier.

CHAPTER 27

PEDICAB: ALSO KNOWN AS A CYCLE RICKSHAW, A THREE-WHEELED BICYCLE ON WHICH A DRIVER, USUALLY IN THE FRONT, PEDALS TO CARRY A PASSENGER

A boombox rests at the foot of a hip hop street performer, dancing and beatboxing. The Santa Monica Pier is full of people of every color and nationality in shorts, bathing suits, costumes, and work clothes. Muscle men, rollerbladers, street musicians, and artists blend into the carnival-like setting. A group of about seventy bicycles and riders circle Topper sitting on the front of a bike carriage, painted in bright East Indian colors with silk curtains, the Route 66 *End of the Road* behind him. Topper wears white lycra bike shorts, a white tank top, a Freddy Mercury-inspired stretch yellow jacket with many buckles, and a white feather boa.

The crowd hears a loud car honk and looks to the street to see a powder blue 1920's Bugatti 35B convertible with Ana in the passenger seat. The car stops, and the driver walks around to open her door. Ana gets out wearing khaki jodhpurs, a white linen blouse, leather boots, a pith helmet with a silky floral scarf around it and her chin, and large sunglasses.

She waves dramatically to the crowd on the bikes. They cheer along with many others on the street.

Topper walks over, kisses her, and unfastens her vintage valise strapped to the back of the car. Some press is taking photos, and many people in the crowd have cameras as well. Ana and Topper walk to the carriage, and Topper pulls the curtains back. Ana climbs in and remains standing. Topper hands her a microphone and gets onto the bike.

"My darlings," she says poised and confidently, waving her hand like royalty.

The crowd cheers.

"We embark on a historic journey. The car you see here, this beautiful blue Bugatti, was made for two things. Racing and making love in the countryside."

The crowd whistles and cheers more loudly.

"It was never intended to sit in five hours of traffic every day."

More applause.

"Put away your cars, dear ones. Put them away, shall we?!" Ana sits down in the bike carriage. "Onward!"

As the onlookers cheer, Topper pedals out of the Pier and down the street with the biking followers close behind.

CHAPTER 28

ODOMETER: CALCULATES SPEED AND DISTANCE AND, IN THE CASE OF MODERN CYCLOCOMPUTERS, EVERYTHING ABOUT LIFE ON THE BICYCLE

Tilly and Camas ride along the shore of Lake Coeur d'Alene with a few dozen riders following behind them on the highway.

"Nice job getting the Seattle mayor to commit to the tulips."

"I took a negotiation class. You need to ask for the order, sista."

Tilly answers her watch phone, "Hey, Max."

"I see you've picked up some friends."

"Yes, some are from Seattle, and a few have joined since then."

"It adds some liability, but you'll be more visible both for safety and the cause."

"They're nice. It's sweet of them to join in," Tilly says.

"There's a group of riders starting from L.A."

"How do you know they're riding for Petal Pedal?"

"There's a flamboyant singer who's blasted it to all her fans."

"Well, I'll be god damned," Camas says.

Rock is sitting at a conference table in the Gold Knights offices where owners, Koby Bounty and Fergie Ripen, show him the investment rating tool.

"It's ready to launch. You just have to figure out how to promote it," Koby says.

"I've got that figured out, I think," Rock replies. "We'll promote it within our firm, and that alone will get the word out. We'll also do some ads."

"We'll include it in the next magazine as well," Fergie adds.

"Thanks, guys. Good job."

"Aren't you friends with the woman doing the cross-country bike ride for the bicycle?" Koby asks.

"Yes, Tilly came to see me a few months ago. She and her bike-partner asked a lot of pointed questions about oil."

"Like what?"

"How to bring it down."

The Gold Knights owners look at each other and raise their eyebrows.

"There are some people taking notice. A friend from the Detroit newspaper said some anonymous folks are taking out ads to mock them," Koby says.

"I don't doubt it," Rock responds, shaking his head.

"Oil brought down by a couple of bikes. It's more than a long shot."

"I remember two young bucks excited about a magazine with a dream to save the world. Nobody thought that would work either."

The two nod and smile.

CHAPTER 29

FAT TIRE BIKE: A BIKE WITH TIRES 3.8 TO OVER FIVE INCHES MADE FOR SNOW, BIKEPACKING, SAND, OR JUST TO SMOOTH OUT A RIDE WITHOUT SUSPENSION

A steep uphill highway with tall forest on either side stretches ahead of Tilly and Camas with the bike followers behind.

"Damn, this road is a son of a bitch. It's hella steep and boring."

"We'll be in Missoula tonight. Luuk and Plume have set up a concert, remember?"

"Thank goodness... a mini break," Camas says as she stands on her pedals to have the power to climb the agonizingly steep hill.

Tilly, behind her, pulls out a whistle and blows it at regular, sharp intervals.

Camas turns around, "Very funny." She doesn't smile.

"I've been dying to do that." Tilly laughs then starts in again.

Camas can't help but laugh. The other riders are confused by the whistle sounds but enjoy seeing Tilly and Camas having fun. The followers smile and laugh along.

The group reaches the summit then joyfully coasts down the hill, enjoying the respite. They ride past the beautiful Clark Fork River, over an old bridge, and through the quaint mountain town of St. Regis, population 300. There is a small group of twenty people, mostly women, standing in front of their tiny post office with mountain bikes, road bikes, and city cruisers. A couple of children with training wheels have tagged along. They cheer as they see Tilly and Camas approaching.

"Welcome!"

"Thank you!" Tilly smiles.

A woman, in her forties, wearing mountain bike clothes, a bandana under her helmet, and fingerless gloves, who appears to be a leader in the cycle group, pulls a manifesto and town bike first plan out of her backpack.

"We don't have a mayor here, just a small town council, but we want you to know that we've started implementing our bike first plan." She points. "See our tulips there?!"

She points to a round garden at the corner across the street with a vintage bike sculpture in the center. On the sculpture is a sign, 'This is a bike and pedestrian town. Share the road. Slow down and leave 3 feet.'

"We've stenciled a bike path to the school, and we plan to do the entire town."

"That won't take long," Camas says under her breath.

"A local business has donated some tall markers that we'll install this summer before the next school year. We'll be able to see the bike lane when it snows."

"It's wonderful!" Tilly says.

"Can some of us ride with you to Missoula?"

"Of course!"

The other rider-followers come out of the town market. The townspeople greet them, and they make friendly, boisterous, introductions. A woman with a large camera with a long lens takes photos of the group talking and Tilly and Camas getting on their bikes, then heading down the road with about fifty riders in tow.

CHAPTER 30

SEATPOST CLAMP: THE COLLAR LOCATED AT THE TOP OF THE SEAT TUBE ON THE FRAME, WHICH HOLDS THE SEATPOST AT THE DESIRED HEIGHT

"I know, daddy," Goosey says in a whiney, almost crying voice. "It's not fair."

"I haven't seen you this upset since you had that plastic surgery mishap and had to find one temporary bosom," her father says.

"There's no need to bring my bosom into this."

"Sorry."

"First, Rock starts that damn color wheel of hell, then those hippie biker chicks are getting people hell-bent against the car, and now the board is asking me to step down as CEO."

"Maybe it has something to do with the fact that you said you'd like to see those girls fly off the edge of the Grand Canyon into a uranium mine to a reporter."

"Possibly. In any case, I called some of our friends. People who would not be happy either if people ride bikes instead of drive cars."

"Goosey, be careful."

"We're going to run some print ads to educate people. Maybe do some TV too."

"I just don't want to see my daughter on TV in an orange jumpsuit."

Camas dances wildly in front of a stage with a band as Plume circles her in expressive, ecstatic-dance-style. There is a *Great Petal Pedal Ride* sign behind the band, and potted tulips decorate the front of the stage.

"Nice tulips!" Camas shouts over the music to Plume.

"People in Missoula brought those," Plume shouts back.

"Wow!"

Tilly stands across the park, talking on her phone.

"How's everything in Napa?" Tilly asks.

"Things are moving along," Ella answers, standing in front of the elementary school, waiting to pick up her daughter. "We're gaining momentum, and people hearing about your ride helps!"

"Awesome. I wanted to thank you for the great job you did on the small city bike plan. I love the community building road map. That's been so useful for all three plans."

"There was a steep learning curve, for sure. We're still learning."

"Yes, we are," Tilly responds.

Ella clears her throat, then reads dramatically from the manifesto. "Today, with gyroscopic momentum, we roll across these paths and roads under our own power from the Pacific coast of Washington State to Washington DC on a bicycle. We ride for children making their way to school safely on bikes."

"Yes! Hey, I've got to run. I've got an appointment to read that in a few minutes on stage!"

"Go! Talk soon!"

A Missoula television reporter stands in front of a long rack of bikes with the live music behind.

"I'm here at Bonner Park in Missoula, where a large group of cyclists and others are here for a concert to welcome The Great Petal Pedal Ride and its founders Tilly and Camas. The ride started in La Push, Washington..."

Big Three CEO Daddy Oilbucks, a heavyset man in his sixties, bald on top, wearing a large black suit with a white shirt and dark tie, stands behind his desk in a luxurious office with vintage and new car posters of iconic car brands on the wall. He watches the news report about the Petal Pedal Ride, shakes his head with an angry red face, and slams his fist down on a newspaper with a picture of Tilly and tulips on the cover. He opens the paper and sees an insert with the route map and the manifesto. He holds the insert up for a moment, reads a portion, then tears it violently, balling it up and throwing it angrily across the room.

CHAPTER 31

BANANA BIKE: ALSO CALLED A WHEELIE BIKE, MUSCLE BIKE, HIGH-RISER, OR SPYDER BIKE, A 60'S CHILDREN'S BICYCLE DESIGNED TO RESEMBLE A CHOPPER MOTORCYCLE

From L.A. to Flagstaff, Ana quickly grew followers on social media and the highway as she elegantly maneuvered publicity in a *movie-star-like montage*.

Elmer's Bottle Tree Ranch, Oro Grande, California ⁻ Ana wears a Natalie Wood inspired space-girl outfit, silver western blouse, silver shorts with a wide 4-inch cinched belt, silver cowboy boots with a silver cowboy hat and poses for a photo in front of the orchard of bottle trees. Topper, wearing a tight fitted tulip Petal Pedal Ride T-shirt and cuffed Levis, posts the photo on his phone.

Cool Springs Gas Station, between Oatman and Kingman ⁻ Arizona ⁻ Ana stands in front of the retro gas station wearing a classic red and white gingham-checked square dance dress with western yoke and flouncy white and red embroidered skirt with red cowboy boots. Topper types on his phone, posting the photo.

Snow Caps Drive Inn, Seligman, Arizona - Ana stands on the roof next to the neon snow cone sign as the bicycle followers pose standing in front of the drive-inn. She wears a movie-star version of animated-Jessie's cowgirl costume, a red flat-brimmed hat with white-laced edge, a white and yellow-yoked western shirt with yellow cuffs, cow print chaps over high-waisted jeans, with a big western belt buckle and brown cowboy boots. Topper snaps the shot and posts the photo.

Grand Canyon Railway Train, Williams, Arizona - Ana poses in front of the dramatic Grand Canyon rim with her arms outstretched upwards in a 1930's Hollywood-inspired cowgirl costume, a striped western blouse with bolo tie, high-waisted vintage jeans, a cowboy hat and matching boots. Topper photographs her and quickly posts the photo.

Tilly and Camas walk into the Western Café in Bozeman, Montana, a retro diner with a taxidermy assortment and antlers on the wall and a stuffed Grizzly standing in the corner. A breakfast counter lines the wall with stainless steel trimmed diner stools and walls covered in knotty pine paneling.

"Howdy pardner," Camas says to the stuffed grizzly as she walks in the door.

A man sitting at the counter smiles and says, "Howdy, missy!"

Tilly reads an old newspaper article on the wall. "Look, it says this place was purchased for $49 in 1871."

They greet a few fellow riders in the café and walk to a booth in the corner. A friendly waitress takes their order. Tilly puts the band of her watch on a ketchup bottle and dials Max.

"Well, hello, gorgeous," Ana says to a life-size Elvis statue as she and Topper walk into Mister D'z, a 1950's classic Route 66 diner. The décor is bright pink and teal with a black and white checkered floor. Two vintage gas pumps filled with candy are standing next to Elvis.

She and Topper sit down at a table, and a waitress takes their order. Ana answers a video call on her phone.

"Ana, thank you so much for taking this call. I have Tilly and Camas on the line," Max says.

"Hello, darlings," Ana says.

Camas looks over at Tilly with a quizzical look.

"Thank you for allowing me on your call. This is my partner, Topper."

"Hello," Topper says.

"It's so great to meet you, Ana. I can't tell you how grateful we are that you're leading the group from L.A.," Max says.

Ana walks to the door of the café and points her phone towards the outside. "I'm not sure if you can see, but we have about 200 bikes with us and more join every day."

"It's fantastic! And all that you are doing on social media

is also causing folks to join our group, and take action in the towns and cities," Tilly adds.

Camas looks a little perturbed at all the praise being showered on Ana.

"Yes, Ana. That Grand Canyon photo was epic," Plume adds.

"Thank you so much. Did you know that Theodore Roosevelt and John Muir rode that train? Well, not at the same time. More importantly, it keeps 50,000 cars out of the park each year."

"Ana, we wanted you to be on this call because we're going to talk about how we're going to get every town on board for June 4th," Max says.

"What's June 4th?" Ana asks,

"Good question," Max responds.

Camas rolls her eyes.

"That's the Bike First Car Out event date," Max says.

"We've got the universe of cities and towns," Bram says.

"Bram! How are you?!" Tilly exclaims.

"The gang's all here, Luuk, Fenna, Plume, Samprati, Sharu, Graeme, Liz, Mayor Dandy, Ella and Mayor Patrick," says Bram.

"Hi everybody! Miss you all!" Tilly says excitedly.

"How are you doing?" Graeme asks.

Tilly turns to Camas, "How are we doing?"

"It's fucking hard," Camas says. "That's what it is. We need to make sure these towns get the message if we're doing all of this god damn riding in ghost towns and shit. My ass is sore."

"Camas, Topper here. I'll overnight chafing cream to you. It works wonders." Topper says warmly. Ana puts her hand on his and smiles.

"That's why we're here, Camas," Max says. "Well, not about your derriere. I am sorry it's sore, though," he says sincerely. "Bram and Luuk, will you update us on the plan, please?"

"Ana, I am such a huge fan of yours. I saw you perform in London at Wembley in 2005," Luuk says.

"Thank you, darling."

"It was so amazing. And your fabulous costumes..." Luuk goes on.

Camas turns her head away from the phone camera, "Kill me," under her breath.

Bram clears his throat.

Luuk realizes he has interrupted the meeting. "Oh, so sorry."

Bram continues, "Tilly, we have scheduled live meetings for you and Camas from here to Chicago. Ana, if you would like to participate too, Fenna will join you on live calls on your route."

"Yes, we would." She looks at Topper, and he smiles lovingly at her.

"Great!"

"There will be live streaming shows on all the social networks promoted along the route. Anyone, city official or layman, can watch any or all of the shows," Plume explains.

Luuk continues, "In the show, Tilly or Ana will present the manifesto and plan. We've put together a media blitz to promote the live meetings and a volunteer center to call and email all of the officials before the show to extend a personal invitation."

"Wow, who organized the call center," Tilly asks.

"Ella spearheaded that, and Sharu and Samprati are organizing the data."

"Nice work!" Mayor Dandy says.

"Yeah, terrific, Ella," Tilly says.

"Graeme, Liz, and I are cueing up the largest cities, New

York, San Francisco, Los Angeles, Chicago etc. We'll be calling on you as we have these meetings set up," Bram says.

"The goal for these manifesto meetings, of course, is for every town and city to commit to a Bike First Car Out event on June 4th. How does that sound, ladies, and Topper," Max asks.

"A delightful challenge! May we please get some manifestos," Ana asks.

"Yes, the L.A. Times and some other papers printed the ride and the manifesto as an insert, and we got a million additional copies printed. We'll make sure they get to you asap," Plume says.

"Thank you, lovely."

"Oh, Ana, thank you. We are so honored that you're a part of this Great Petal Pedal Ri..."

Interrupting Plume, "Right on, Max. Hey, thanks... everyone... for your hard work," Camas says in no-nonsense, business-like voice.

"You two beautiful, strong women riders are the ones doing the heavy lifting," Liz says.

"Damn right. OK, I'm going to eat some of these cowboy chicken fried steak calories now. Signing off."

"Be safe out there," Max calls before Camas hangs up.

Camas digs purposefully into her breakfast, not looking up at Tilly.

"What's up with you?" Tilly asked. "You weren't very friendly."

"Holy shit. Everybody was falling all over themselves for that Ana Bananarama."

"You have to admit that it's pretty cool that she's the Pied Piper of L.A. and bringing all those riders."

"Her ass is on a cushion," Camas says as she takes a huge bite of chicken fried steak and gravy.

CHAPTER 32

ACTION CAMERA: A SMALL VIDEO CAMERA THAT CAN BE MOUNTED ON BICYCLE HANDLEBARS, HELMET OR OTHER SAFE LOCATIONS

Rock sits at a large table in the private dining room of a classic, high end steakhouse in downtown Detroit. Dark burgundy wallpaper covers the walls, the ceiling is painted gold, and a large crystal chandelier hangs over the 12-seat dining table. The room is surrounded by floor-to-ceiling glass-doored cabinets full of expensive wine from all over the world. Next to Rock is Big Three CEO Madame, an elegant woman in her fifties in a simple long-sleeve black dress and pearls. Across the table is Daddy Oilbucks and Big Three CEO Brit, a middle-aged, handsome man with a brunette beard and mustache, trim-figured in a well-cut dark suit, black shirt, and tie.

"What gives me this distinct pleasure to be having lunch with all of you?" Rock asks brightly.

"We had to invite you, so it doesn't appear that we're colluding or price-fixing," says Oilbucks.

"Ah, those darn ol' antitrust laws," Rock replies.

"We did want to hear how your energy rater scheme is going," Madame adds.

A waiter brings bourbon on the rocks to Oilbucks, a vodka martini with two olives to Madame, a glass of red wine to Brit, and an amber beer to Rock.

"It isn't a scheme, but yes, I'm happy to fill you in."

"If it redistributes wealth from me to you, then I call that a scheme," Madame responds dryly.

Rock lifts his glass, "Cheers."

They toast, and the waiter begins to take their order.

"I'll have the trout," Rock says.

CHAPTER 33

BRAZE-ONS: THREADED SOCKETS THAT MAY OR MAY NOT BE PRESENT ON THE BIKE FRAME THAT PROVIDE A PLACE TO ATTACH ACCESSORIES

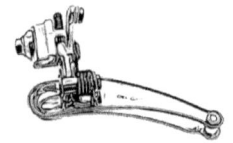

S haru and Samprati work diligently at their computers at the Burning Man offices. Max paces and talks to them, occasionally answering his phone to take a call. The computer screens show the GIS location of Tilly and Ana and varying-sized dots of all of the towns and cities. As they get a "yes" to bike first, they mark the city in green, along with a running-total counter for the total cities and total population committed in a highlighted box on the screen.

On the wall, hung very high, is a large, framed black and white photograph of two suffragette-era women riding their bicycles. Below it, above eye level, is a sign that reads *32,000 towns and cities* on the left and *328,240,000 people* on the right with clips underneath. A standing height drawing table nearby holds a feather quill pen, a jar of black ink, and a stack of white paper. Sharu picks up the pen and paper and writes a large "1" and clips it under *towns and cities*, then "300" on another piece and clips it under *population*.

As Ana continues to broadcast Petal Pedal power, posing

with her bike entourage at beautiful painted desert locations with quaint, colorful adobe cottages in Flagstaff, Gallop, Albuquerque, and Santa Fe, Tilly and Camas are busy holding the live-streamed mayor meetings in historic city halls, modern buildings, public spaces, cafes, and living rooms.

"I think this must be the most boring road in the United States," Camas says.

"I think it's pretty. We saw the Big Horn Mountains back there. The mesas and sagebrush are lovely, and the sky is so big and blue," Tilly responds.

"You think everything is pretty."

"Not everything. Not those oil fields back in Cody."

"All I can see are cows and tumbling tumbleweeds." Camas pauses, thinking. "That's it. I need weed!"

"I don't think it's legal here."

"Godforsaken country."

"We only have 42 miles to Casper."

Ana's route looks exotic with," pausing for effect, "... people."

"We'll have plenty of people eventually, and Casper looks like a fun honky-tonk town. We have these lovely friends on the road with us too."

"True. They are cool."

The riders behind them are enjoying themselves, talking, and laughing.

"Did you know that Detroit is just 260 miles from Chicago?" Tilly asks.

"That's not on our route."

"Ana has a musician friend who's playing at the Americas Worldwide Automobile Show."

"That's not on our route."

"What are the chances that our ride is passing through during the biggest auto show in the world?"

"We're not passing through."

CHAPTER 34
CHAIN WHIP: USED IN CONJUNCTION WITH A CASSETTE REMOVING TOOL TO REMOVE THE LOCKRING OF A CASSETTE FROM THE FREEHUB BODY, OR A TRACK COG FROM A HUB

The two large flocks of cyclists fly past city and town welcome signs like a flip chart of classic vintage tourist postcards with *Greetings from...* , the letters filled with images of sight-seeing points of interest.

Greetings from Amarillo, Texas... Ana, Topper, and the mayor of Amarillo sit at a picnic table in front of Cadillacs with their front ends in the ground and tails in the air at the Cadillac Ranch. Many riders' bicycles are propped up against the cars in contrast.

Greetings from Chadron, Nebraska... Tilly and Camas are in pedal-boats in picturesque Chadron State Park. The mayor of Chadron pedals along with Tilly. She shows him the bike plan and they have an animated discussion as Camas flirts with a male passenger in her boat.

Greetings from Catoosa, Oklahoma... Ana and the Mayor of Catoosa pose for a photo in front of the large open mouth whale on Route 66. The mayor holds up a manifesto in one hand and gives the thumbs up in the other.

"We're actually here to talk about how best to stop the momentum of that, what is it called, the pesky puta ride?" Brit says, putting a large piece of steak in his mouth and washing it down with a big drink of red wine.

"Petal Pedal Ride. The Great Petal Pedal Ride, to be exact," Rock says.

"My marketing VP says it's all over the world wide web," Oilbucks says, enunciating the high tech words slowly and carefully with a stern face.

"Don't upset yourself. Enjoy your lunch," Madame says calmly with an icy tone.

"All I know is that car sales are down in the Netherlands, and that is a country full of bikes," Brit says.

"Yes, that is about all you know," Oilbucks jabs sarcastically, "but don't you have any ideas?"

"Ms. Butimines called me and suggested some well placed educational advertisements."

"Don't try to pretend you're at arm's length with her, pleeeeeeease," Madame says.

"Is anyone?" Rock adds. "I don't see how defaming two idealistic young women is going to solve anything."

All three look up from their lunches with a horrified look.

Greetings from Des Moines, Iowa... Tilly, Camas, and the mayor of Des Moines ride through the colorful Pappajohn Sculpture Park on bikes.

Greetings from St. Louis, Missouri. Ana and Topper eat custard with the mayor of St. Louis at Ted Drewes Frozen Custard on Route 66. The herd of riders following Ana and Topper ride through St. Louis with the dramatic Gateway Arch in the distance.

Tulips become more plentiful in all of the towns and cities they pass through as the Petal Pedal Ride gets closer and closer to the windy city. Across the globe, beautiful tulips erupt in the city of Utrecht and the Netherland countryside. Bicycle riders increase in numbers, coming from all directions toward Chicago, joining the group rides, all with some type of tulip representation, tulip T-shirts, tulip bouquets, tulip phone cases, tulip hats, and tulip tattoos.

"Your bogus sustainability tool was an unwelcome surprise, Rock, but protecting these hippy-radical-earth-huggers, is unconscionable," Madame says.

"You're hanging on a thread. These millennials are not impressed by status or money, and they're pissed off that we've taken a crap on any chance of a living planet. Do you think the next generation is just going to wake up and say, 'Sorry mom and dad, I want a two-ton mega SUV,'?" Rock says.

"The United States is not going back to the cold, the dark,

and the bicycle," Oilbucks roars, his face red, as he signs the credit card receipt.

"Thanks for lunch," Brit says to Oilbucks.

"Yes, thank you," Madame adds.

They look at Rock.

"Why, thank you for this delicious lunch. Oh, by the way, did you see that dry age room full of dead carcasses on the way in? Goodness, if someone took out this restaurant, between all the industrial-farmed cows and oil, we'd save the planet in one fell swoop!" Rock gets up and walks out with a nod of his head. "Good day."

Tilly, Camas, and the group of rider-followers turn down a road and are greeted by members of the Rosebud Reservation in traditional tribal dress. They hold tulips and excitedly welcome Tilly, Camas, and the others as they arrive. One of the elders presents a hawk feather to Tilly with a reverent bow of her head. The riders pull into a large field and begin setting up their tents.

Tilly and Camas sit outside their tents in front of a campfire with the moon and a sky full of bright stars overhead. There is tribal dancing, chanting around a larger fire in the distance.

"Checking in on you," Max says from Tilly's watch screen.

"We're doing great. We had a lovely welcome from the Rosebud Sioux Tribe."

"Yeah, it was nice," Camas says impatiently. "What does the ad say?"

"I'm not sure you want to know," Max responds.

"Yes, we do," Camas says.

"'Two radical hippie girls are riding bikes trying to take away your freedoms.'"

The irony of the word freedoms and the chanting and dancing of the native peoples in the background are not lost on the young women.

"They want to take away your car. Your freedom to drive this beautiful country. Your freedom to travel and take your family vacations. Your freedom to drive to work and not sit in crime on a commuter train. Stop them, so they don't stop you!' That last line is very large, with an exclamation point."

"Gosh," Tilly says weakly.

"And it has beautiful pictures of our national parks next to picture of a dirty subway with people of color."

"Mother fuckers," Camas says.

CHAPTER 35

SAFETY FLAG: A REFLECTIVE BANNER OF CLOTH OR PLASTIC AT THE END OF A TALL FLEXIBLE POLE ATTACHED TO A BIKE TO INCREASE VISIBILITY IN TRAFFIC

Ana Chronism's bike group, followed by Tilly DeMontagne's, over 1,000 people total on bicycles, ride down Michigan Avenue along Lake Michigan to Daley Plaza full of a cheering crowd of people with bikes. The crowd is totally tuliped-out with tulips in their hands, tulips in their helmets, and wearing Great Petal Pedal Ride T-shirts. Ana and her group arrive first. She is high in the air on an antique bicycle with a giant front wheel wearing a late 1800's suffragette costume. Topper's carriage is pulling her bicycle, so she doesn't topple over. The crowd cheers and hands tulips to Ana and the other riders as they ride to the front of the large Picasso sculpture. Ana waves regally to the crowd.

When the spectators see Tilly and Camas, they cheer wildly. Sarah, a pretty, waif-like, young woman in her twenties, with fair skin and wire-rimmed glasses, and a political button reading *Refill, Bill*, steps out and hugs Tilly as she walks past.

"Sarah! How's DC?"

Sarah gives her the thumbs as Tilly gets pulled away by the crowd flow.

There is a group of protesters on the periphery with signs reading, "Go back home!" "Cars are freedom," "I gas guzzle because I can," "Bikes make my fat ass hurt."

"It's being called the 'path of petals.' The Great American Petal Pedal Ride has reached downtown Chicago, and what started as two riders, Tilly DeMontagne and her best friend, has turned into about 500 riders plus another 600 riders arriving from along the historic Route 66. The number of riders has been growing daily as they travel towards the nation's capital. Sharon is at Daley Plaza reporting live. Sharon?"

"Tilly just arrived, and it's pandemonium as the bike riders shout and cheer behind me. We're watching as Tilly meets singer Ana Chronism for the first time. The crowd is very excited. The riders are introducing themselves, hugging, exchanging small gifts. There's a group of protesters on the edge of the crowd with pro car signs. So close to the auto capital of Detroit, I hope everything stays peaceful here."

"What's that they're chanting?"

"June 4th bikes first. That's the day they are asking every town and city to close streets to cars. Back to you, Bob."

"No wonder there are protesters!"

Tilly and Camas ride up to Ana and Topper as Topper helps Ana down from the tall bike. Tilly hands Camas her bike as she rushes over to shake Ana's hand, then Ana pulls her in for a hug. Tilly embraces Ana with a huge smile, then hugs Topper.

"So great to finally meet you in person!" Tilly says.

"My pleasure, darling," Ana says graciously.

"Very cool bike. Nice entrance!" Tilly adds.

"Hi, great job," Camas says with a meager smile, extending her hand.

"You too, beautiful," Ana says.

Camas shrugs off the compliment.

"I set up the meeting in Detroit," Ana says to Tilly over the crowd noise and people pushing in to meet them.

Camas overhears, does a double-take, then turns away in anger. Crowds are swarming them.

"Let's go, Cam. Time to get onstage for the manifesto," Tilly says, trying to reach Camas as she walks away.

Tilly grabs her arm. "Cam! It's over this way."

"You planned the Detroit trip even when Max and I said it didn't make sense?" Camas says strongly.

"I think it's importa..."

"I think you and Ana can do the manifesto on stage. She seems to be your new confidante and the big star with all the fans anyway. I don't even have a name around her." She continues walking. "I'm just the 'best friend,' and now I'm not sure I'm even that!" Camas walks into the crowd with her bike.

"Camas! Cam!!" Tilly calls to her. "We finally made it to Chicago! Please!"

Ana takes Tilly's arm. "They're motioning for you to get on stage."

"Let's go together," Tilly says distractedly, as she looks for Camas in the crowd.

A Chicago funk band plays on stage as the mayor, Ana and Topper sing along and dance. Tilly is worried, but she puts on a good face, smiling as she shuffles her feet and moves her arms a bit, looking out into the crowd for Camas.

Camas can hear the words of the manifesto as she makes her way through the plaza crowd.

"We ride for my mother and father to ride a bicycle without fear of being crushed under the wheels of a passing truck."

Tilly suddenly stops, grimaces, as she flashes back. *A couple on a windy mountain road. The logging truck bearing down on them.* She starts to faint and stumbles. Topper catches her. The crowd gasps.

"Do you need to sit?!" Topper asks with concern.

"No, no. I'm fine. Probably just the long ride," Tilly says, shaking her head and taking a deep breath.

Ana hands her the mic and smiles encouragingly.

Tilly stands up straight and speaks confidently. "We ride for our grandparents to ride to the market to buy vegetables for their supper, flowers for a neighbor, then safely home again..."

Tilly lifts her bike onto the baggage platform as she checks into a flight with a backpack and panniers. She runs to her gate.

CHAPTER 36

DROP BAR: THE TYPE OF HANDLEBAR FOUND ON ROAD RACING BIKES, WITH THE HALF-CIRCLE-SHAPED CURVED ENDS THAT EXTEND BELOW THE TOP PART OF THE BAR

Camas drinking a 20-ounce beer and eats a heaping plate of fried appetizers in the Chicago hotel lounge

"Camas!" Liam calls out happily.

Camas turns around to see Liam and Pedro walking into the lounge.

"Wow, hi!" she says as she hugs Liam, then squats down to give Pedro a squeeze.

"This is a surprise. Have you seen Tilly yet?"

"No, she's not answering my texts. I'm a little worried."

Camas calls Max from her watch. "Max, we're trying to find Tilly. Can you check the GPS."

"She's in her hotel room as far as I can tell. I just assumed she was exhausted and slept all day."

"Shit!"

Camas jumps up and runs out of the bar. Liam and Pedro follow close behind. She runs down the hotel stairs as fast as she can to the parking garage. She races across the garage to the van and stops, looking at the trailer.

"Her bike's gone."

The three race back up the stairs at full speed to the eighth floor, then down the hall and rush into the room. Camas grabs the blanket off of Tilly's bed and lifts her pillow to find Tilly's GPS watch and a note.

My best friend Camas, I'll meet you in Akron. Please don't worry. Lead the riders. Love, Tilly.

Camas runs down the hall and pounds on Ana and Topper's door. Liam and Pedro run up just as Ana opens the door wearing a glamorous long satin robe. She has a matching satin sleep mask pulled up to her hairline, her hair flowing beautifully as if just styled.

"Where is she?!" Camas says forcefully.

"Pardon me?"

"She's gone! Tilly's gone. Her bike's gone too," Camas says frantically. "Did she go to Detroit?"

"She didn't tell me."

"If she went, where would she be?!"

"My friend, Dustin Laekinwood, is playing at the Auto Show Charity Gala tonight. She might be going there."

"Damn it, Ana. You sent her into a wolves' den."

"When you and Max advised against it, I told her that we should stay on the route."

"She didn't listen obviously," Camas says dryly.

"That's why she's leading us."

"I've got to find her!" Camas pleads.

"I think you can still catch a flight out if you hurry."

"Can you lead the riders, and we'll meet you in Akron?"

"Yes."

"I'm coming with you," Liam says.

"What about P?" Camas asks.

Shasta races in and stands in the hotel doorway. "I'll watch him!"

"Thanks!" Camas says, and she gives her a high five as she runs out the door. "Let's go!"

Liam runs after her, handing Pedro to Shasta.

CHAPTER 37

HUB: THE CENTRAL COMPONENT OF A WHEEL; INSIDE THE HUB ARE THE AXLE AND BALL BEARINGS

Loved by liberals and conservatives alike, big-name, male pop artist, Dustin Laekinwood, dances and sings to a Motown song with a hip hop vibe played by his eight-piece band with three back-up singers. It is the last song of his show at the end of the Auto Show Charity Gala in a 40,000 square foot ballroom with dinner tables of several hundred guests. Dustin, in his early thirties with brown short curly hair and a goatee, waves to the crowd as he runs offstage at the end of the song. The well-heeled crowd cheers loudly.

As the crowd continues to applaud and shouts for an encore, he walks back on stage leading Tilly by the hand. Many in the crowd gasp but continue their applause.

"Thanks again for having me."

The crowd quiets.

"This is my friend Tilly DeMontagne. She'd like to say a few words."

Offstage, the event organizer, a short, older, bald man with a mustache in a tuxedo, shouts to the backstage crew, "What?"

Goosey Bitumines gasps from her table. A reporter is filming. Dustin hands the mic to Tilly.

"Hello, I'm Tilly DeMontagne."

The crowd is completely silent. Many look at each other with a quizzical look. Some look angry.

"You may have seen that we've traveled here on bicycles and are headed to Washington DC. I was saddened to read some of the things about us in your papers because we love this country as much as you do, and that includes Detroit."

The event organizer begins to come out on the stage to retrieve Tilly, but Dustin holds his arm firmly and leads him back offstage. Tilly sees Dustin talking to him pointedly and pauses. The crowd is mumbling, and it begins to get louder.

"Get off the stage!" a man shouts from the crowd.

Tilly is a deer in the headlights. She continues slowly, "And then I saw that this big shindig, the reason you all get dressed up, is for kids. It says here in your program..." she stops, "that..."

The crowd is getting restless.

Liam and Camas run through the backstage to the edge of the curtain and see that Tilly is struggling.

Camas runs onstage, grabs the program from Tilly, and takes over reading very loudly, "C.S. Mott Children's Hospital, Boys & Girls Clubs of Southeastern Michigan, Boys Hope Girls Hope Detroit, Children's Center, The Children's Foundation, and it says right here in your program that since 1976, the Charity Gala has raised more than $121 million for Southeastern Michigan children's charities. That's fuckin' awesome."

The crowd's eyes widen. A couple of older men look perturbed.

Goosey yells, "Why are they on the stage!"

Tilly continues tentatively, "That is awesome, and you

should all be so very proud of that accomplishment." She pauses, nervous.

Tilly looks to Camas, who nods a go ahead look.

"...but what you might not be so proud of is that those kids can't ride to school safely on their bikes. Just in the last couple of years, a few people in this city have been killed by cars on their bikes. One a 61-year-old woman, simply on her way to pick up her grandson from school."

Camas jumps in, "My friend's parents were killed on bicycles. Maybe you can't relate to that, but this next one might hit a little closer to home. In your fancy lakeshore town of Grosse Pointe, I think it's the wealthiest town in Michigan, a boy was killed near his high school by a fellow student. One life ended too soon. A second young man who has to live with that the rest of his life. Holy shit."

"Please believe us that we do not want to get rid of cars," Tilly says. "We just need to make bikes our priority. Create a world where all of these children you are trying to help, can ride a bike safely to and from school."

Some of the crowd are murmuring; others look at each other with small nods.

"And you can ride with your children to the market, and your grandchildren to the library, and with your partner to dinner and back. It can be a beautiful life!" Tilly says passionately.

The crowd is looking around. A few old men, including Daddy Oilbucks, stand up to get up to leave, still angry.

"Just where do you think you're going?" Camas shouts, pointing. "Dustin is coming out to play an encore of Rockin' the Casbah country style. I think it's your favorite song. Sit down, Daddy Oilbucks," Camas commands.

They sit back down.

"Yes, hang on please—just one more thing. We have something we'd like to read to you. It won't take long."

"If you want to read along, you can go to "petalpedal.com" flower petal bike pedal dot com," Camas adds.

Dustin comes out and plays a quiet melody on guitar behind Tilly's words.

Tilly clears her throat, "I feel the power of my legs to carry me on this bicycle to smell the fresh air, to buy a sweet, crisp apple that fell from a tree a few miles from here..."

A woman stands and grabs the hand of the woman next to her to pull her up to stand also and recites with Tilly, "...and to sit a spell with you."

Tilly hears words coming from the audience. She realizes some people are reciting. She sees the two women standing. She continues, "Today with gyroscopic momentum, we roll across these paths and roads under our own power from the Pacific coast of Washington State to Washington, DC on a bicycle."

More voices join. More women are standing. Camas joins her, reciting from the stage.

"We ride for children making their way to school safely on bikes..."

Outside on the street, angry crowds are gathering, having found out about Tilly at the gala. Reporters gather too. As Tilly continues, over half the women and a few men are standing and reciting along.

"And during these times, as we ride side-by-side, the car in my garage is as old as me, and the clock will tick until soon the last pipeline full of gas, the last barrel of crude oil, and the last container of coal will leave our mother earth."

Dustin plays a beautiful chord and speaks into the mic to recite the manifesto with Tilly, Camas, and the crowd.

"One city, one country, one continent, one planet united in abundance, peace, harmony, joy, laughter, and love by the world's greatest invention... the bicycle."

The band begins playing Rock the Casbah. Most of the crowd erupts in applause.

Dustin turns to Tilly away from the mic, "My manager just told me there's a bit of a mob scene outside. Be careful."

Tilly hugs Dustin, then Camas. She and Camas run off the stage. Tilly is elated to see Liam after so many weeks. They embrace tenderly and kiss.

Goosey sees Dustin about to get into his tour bus after the show. "Stupid move, Laekinwood! Why in the world did you risk your career for that?"

"I rode my bike everywhere as a kid. I want that for my daughter."

Goosey rolls her eyes and turns away. Dustin bounds up the steps of his tour bus.

CHAPTER 38

HEADLIGHT: A LIGHT AT THE FRONT OF A BICYCLE TO ILLUMINATE THE ROAD AHEAD

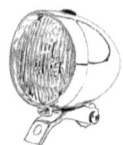

Tilly, Liam, and Camas walk out of the convention center and are mobbed by the press. Angry car-loving bystanders glare and shout, "Go home, hippies!", "Grow up and drive a car, baby!"

"Tilly, are you sure you should have come here? Aren't you afraid of the repercussions?" a report shouts.

"The repercussions of cars are far worse," Tilly calls back as she, Liam, and Camas get on bikes and ride away from the crowd on the city street, the lights of the city and cars leaving the event surrounding them.

Tilly rides in the lead.

Camas behind her, calls out, "You said you wouldn't leave me on the journey."

"I'm pretty sure you left me, but I'm really sorry," Tilly says sincerely.

"You kicked ass up there."

"Thanks, friend. You too. Thanks for saving me."

"Car back! There's a car on my ass. Stay over. Be careful," Liam shouts.

"It's safer staying a bit in the street," Tilly says. Her face is flush, and she perspires from the stress of the cars.

"I mean it! This asshole is riding me!"

"There's no place to turn out!" Tilly shouts.

Goosey, in a huge Hummer, rides close behind Liam and revs her engine loudly. People are walking down the sidewalk nearby. A young woman takes out her phone to record the aggressive tailgating. Goosey steps on the gas abruptly, passes Liam, honking her horn without ceasing. Her car sideswipes Tilly on her bike, the rearview mirror striking Tilly as it passes by. The bike swerves onto the curb, and Tilly flies off in a roll. She ends up flat on her back.

"Tilly!" Camas shouts in horror.

The people on the sidewalk are aghast. "Are you OK?" "Are you OK?" They repeat.

Camas and Liam rush to her side. The young woman continues to film as Goosey flees the scene.

CHAPTER 39

FLOOR PUMP: POSITIVE-DISPLACEMENT AIR PUMP DESIGNED FOR INFLATING BICYCLE TIRES, USUALLY WITH A CONNECTION OR ADAPTER FOR SCHRADER OR PRESTA VALVES

"How's Tilly?" Max asks Camas from the Burning Man offices.

"Only a few scrapes and bruises."

"She's lucky to be alive. Shasta is calling. The riders are almost to the DuSable Michigan Street bridge. We'll talk later."

Max answers his phone.

"Hey Max, you won't believe it, man." Shasta sounds frantic.

"What is it?"

"The fucking bridge is rising up."

"What?"

"We're a block away, and the bridge is closed. See?"

Shasta points her phone towards the Chicago River. The riders fill the street with nowhere to go. The bridge is open in the center with both sides angled towards the sky.

"I'll reroute you to another bridge," Max says quickly,

looking at his computer. "Go west. You can take the North Wabash bridge."

"I see it." Shasta pauses. "You're not going to believe this."

"What?"

"It's rising up too! I'm looking down the river, and North Wabash is going up. And the next one, and the next!"

Down the river, each bridge is opening up.

"Is there a boat coming through?"

"Nope."

"Bastards."

"There's a slew of cars everywhere. Some have anti bicycle signs, and they're shouting at us. They're creating traffic gridlock."

"Grab Plume."

"I'm here, Max," Plume says attentively.

"We're taking a moment. Please hold hands."

"Thank goodness I've been at Burning Man," Shasta says.

"Take a deep breath."

Plume and Shasta hold hands. They all take a deep breath.

"Mother father universe, we ask that you hold these riders in the light. Help us help them find a safe route onward."

"Fine! Prayer, check. Now figure this fucking thing out, Max!" Shasta commands.

"Stand by. Over and out."

The Petal Pedal Ride team rallies to gather cycling helpers for the blockaded riders in Chicago. Max, Sharu, and Samprati are on their phones and computers calling and emailing. Graeme and Liz sit at a table at Heaven's Brothers, talking on their phones with serious faces. Reeve talks on his phone and types on his computer simultaneously at his bike shop. Mayors Patrick, Bram, and Dandy talk on their phones from their offices. Topper texts on the front of the carriage bike at the front of the group of riders.

Ana stands and sings to the crowd behind her to calm them as they wait.

"You need to break up. Spread the word to follow local bikers when they arrive and to meet at the Green Barn Apple Farm in La Porte, Indiana.

"What local bikers? I don't see anyone." Shasta questions.

"Help's on the way! Spread the word!"

Plume group texts the riders as Shasta stands broadcasting instructions through loudspeakers off the back of the van as bicycle groups made up of individuals of all shapes, colors, and backgrounds cycle down city side streets and lead bikers out.

Older grey-haired women in lycra on their road bikes. Bike messengers on bikes exit an artsy warehouse. MAMIL's, middle-aged men in lycra, riding fast and drafting, take a quick turn to ride into the city. Mountain bikers racing fast down a wooded trail near the lake, take a detour and ride downtown. Some people on kayaks pull in, hop on their bikes and lead riders out. Suit and tie-wearing, athletic businessmen and businesswomen in city high rises, superman-style, rip off their shirt, tie and suit jackets, or Ann Taylor wrap dresses, jump on their road bikes and ride towards the riders. As the Chicago helpers rescue the riders, some ride on sidewalks; others trot on foot with their bikes to escape the gridlock.

A five-year-old girl in an anti-bike vehicle with her father shouting out the window says, "Mommy, why are we mad at the people with the flowers?"

The cyclists eventually begin to merge back together on the outskirts of the city. Finally, in one group again, they give each other high fives and thumbs up, smiling and laughing as they ride down a country road. An old white farmhouse with a large green barn is the backdrop of the meeting place in La Porte, Indiana.

The Petal Pedal riders and the Chicago cyclists celebrate with a band, barbecue, and many adventurous escape tales. As the day of converging cyclical networks, symbiotic strategic solutions, and valiant urban rescues come to a close, stars float in a deep blue sky over a village of tents and bicycles in a quiet alfalfa field.

CHAPTER 40

PARKING RACK: A DEVICE TO WHICH BICYCLES CAN BE SECURELY ATTACHED FOR PARKING PURPOSES

The Gold Knights owners watch an online stock ticker tape on a computer. A vintage Western Union ticker tape with a glass dome ticks away resting nearby on a side table. Koby and Fergie make a video call to Rock.

"The oil stocks are taking a deep dive," Koby says.

"Yes, they are," Rock agrees. "What's that noise. Sounds like ticker tape."

"It is," Fergie answers. "Koby had to have the real thing. He even retrofitted it, so it actually works."

"Wow. Nerds confirmed."

"This all can't be happening due to the new ranking app," Koby says.

"No. It's helped, but someone got footage of Goosey Butimines's hit and run."

"We heard Tilly got hit. It was Goosey?!"

"Yep. I guess we need a new color for the rating app."

Goosey is led into the courthouse in handcuffs, shackles, and an orange jumpsuit.

CHAPTER 41

DERAILER HANGER: A PART OF THE FRAME WHERE THE REAR DERAILLEUR IS ATTACHED, SOMETIMES A PART OF THE FRAME AND SOMETIMES A SEPARATE, REPLACEABLE PIECE

Camas sits at the desk in a Detroit hotel room, working on her laptop, eating a massive plate of french fries, drinking a large beer. There is a knock at the door. Tilly answers it to find Liam standing there. They kiss.

"How are you feeling?"

"Can we go out on the lake?"

"Now?"

"Yes, please."

Liam and Tilly paddle on stand up paddleboards on the Detroit River next to Belle Isle. The beautiful Anna Scripps Whitcomb Conservatory is in view as they glide towards the beach.

"Race you to the beach!" Tilly says as she paddles strongly.

Liam paddles behind her. Tilly reaches the shore first. She

jumps down into the water and wades to the shore. Liam rushes up to get closer, and they kiss.

"Did you let me win?" Tilly says, flirting.

"Maybe. You just fell off your bike, remember?"

They take a dip and swim back to their boards. Tilly climbs onto her board, and Liam climbs on to face her. He has tears in his eyes.

"I'm sorry. I thought I was OK. I just don't understand."

"There's something that I need to tell you."

"Is there someone else?"

She holds his face in her hands. "Of course not."

"What happened then?"

"I wasn't sure at the time. Something came over me at Black Rock City, and I just couldn't go through with the wedding." Tilly pauses. "I've had this time to think about things."

"I'm listening."

"My parents died when I was in college."

"My dad told me that. I always wondered why you never talked about it."

"They were killed by a logging truck while cycling. It was very quick, they say." Tilly lowers her head, crying.

Liam puts his head to touch hers, keeps it there, and whispers, "I'm so sorry."

Very quietly, she continues, "I think I dealt with the accident itself over the years. Learning to cycle for a triathlon was part of getting over it. But when you asked me to marry you, and we were on the playa, I think I had a huge amount of fear come up about being in a forever partnership with you. Not that I don't want you. I do. Just that pain of the most important couple in my life, my mom and dad, who loved each other so much, as I love you... not surviving. It frightened me."

They put their arms around each other's shoulders as they

sit on the board. They kiss deeply. Tilly looks up. She waits for Liam to say something, but he remains quiet.

"Do you have anything to say? Do you think you could forgive me?"

"There's nothing to forgive. I love you. I just have one more question about what you've just told me."

Tilly waits for the question with wide eyes.

"Will you wear the ring I gave you on the rest of the ride?"

"I'll wear it forever," Tilly says with a huge smile.

She pulls Liam into a strong embrace and kisses him. They fall off the board laughing, and their lips find their way to each other, treading water.

CHAPTER 42

RIM: THE OUTER HOOP PART OF A WHEEL, USUALLY MADE OF ALUMINUM, STEEL OR CARBON FIBER

On a country road outside of Akron, Pedro, in a bike trailer pulled by Tilly, Camas, and Liam reunite jubilantly with Ana, Topper, and the Petal Pedal riders. They all travel down country roads of red barns and farmland. Tulips line the front yards of houses they pass, and many people come out to wave. Some shout "Petal Pedal Ride!" and others "June 4th Bike First!"

The unified assembly of cyclists continues towards Washington, DC, the air becoming more electric with excitement with each passing day and the gathering of participation in the June 4th Bike First event. Reporters interview riders who have joined the ride from far and wide.

Greetings from Muncie, Indiana. Max tears off a sheet of paper reading 8,431 cities - 67,004,331 pop to a blank sheet. He writes '12,051 cities - 121,444,100 pop.'

"I joined the Petal Pedal Ride because I've been to Amsterdam and I'd like to live in a bike city. Why not mine?!"

Greetings from Dayton, Ohio. Samprati tears off the old page. He writes '15,040 cities - 154,272,320 pop.'

"The planet won't survive if we don't take drastic

measures. I don't consider riding a bike to be one of them. Just a simple, good start."

Greetings from Columbus, Ohio. Max tears off the old page. He writes '18,249 cities - 187,096,788 pop.'

"I joined The Great Petal Pedal ride because unified voices with a consistent message can make change happen. And I think Tilly's dog, Pedro, is really cute!"

Cities seem to pass more quickly as they get closer and closer to the nation's capital, and the country embraces the feel-good, hopeful spirit of The Great Petal Pedal ride.

Greetings from Pittsburgh, Pennsylvania. '21,443 cities – 219,920,249 pop.'

Greetings from Cumberland, Maryland. '24,790 cities – 252,744,105 pop.'

Greetings from Martinsburg, West Virginia. '26,994 cities – 261,008,459 pop.'

Greetings from McLean, Virginia. '27,211 cities – 285,568,993 pop.'

Max stands at the window of the Burning Man offices as the sun sets behind the Golden Gate Bridge. The numbers roll up... and up... and up... to '31,044 cities - 318,292,661 pop.'

CHAPTER 43
HELMET: DESIGNED TO ATTENUATE IMPACTS TO THE HEAD OF A CYCLIST IN FALLS WHILE MINIMIZING SIDE EFFECTS SUCH AS INTERFERENCE WITH PERIPHERAL VISION

Bands play on side streets, and huge crowds are gathered as the Petal Pedal riders pass through the streets of Washington DC. Ana is back on the tall antique bike wearing a suffragette-inspired hat with a vintage bathing suit, lace leggings, and ballet slippers. As before, Topper's bike is attached in front, keeping her stable. Just as they reach Pennsylvania Avenue, six large limo SUVs with tinted windows begin to encroach on the riders. The vehicles make their way to the front, slowly and carefully.

"What in the world are these road hogs doing?" Camas says, annoyed.

The large SUVs creep along the side of them until three vehicles are far enough ahead to cross the lane to block the cyclists.

"What the f..."

"Darlings, I think someone wants to have a word with us," Ana says as large men exit the vehicles in unison and, like a dance, come to circle the car closest to Tilly. One of the men opens the back seat door.

Tilly and Camas's eyes widen as the crowd on the street, and the riders gasp. The President of the United States, a tall African American woman in her 40's, gets out of the car. She wears aviator sunglasses, a white linen A-line skirt, a white linen blouse with a navy and white striped cotton sweater on top, white bucks, short lace socks, and a flat brim straw hat, reminiscent of a turn of the century tennis player.

"Madame President, you look marvelous!" Ana calls out.

The crowd and riders are taking photos and sharing them with friends and family.

"Welcome to Washington, DC. We've been expecting you!" The president says with open arms and a beautiful warm smile.

"Thank you, Madame President," Tilly responds with a gentle bow-nod-curtesy. The others follow suit with broad smiles.

Camas walks right up and shakes the president's hand firmly. The bodyguards rush in quickly, but the president waves them away.

"Thank you for being here today," Camas says.

"Well, I do live here."

The crowd laughs.

"May I ride the last few yards with you?" the president asks as a bodyguard takes a bike off of the back of the vehicle. It is a Worksman Dutchie 'Brooklyn' single speed, made by the oldest bike manufacturer in the U.S., and has a basket on the front filled with real tulips.

Incredulous, Tilly and Camas say in unison, "Of course!"

Bodyguards on bicycles ride in formation to surround the president, Tilly, Camas, Ana, and Topper as they start to ride. The Petal Pedal riders resume riding behind them.

When they get to the iconic National Mall on Pennsylvania Avenue, the president, flanked by Tilly and Camas on the left and Ana and Topper on the right, begins speaking. Her bicycle has a microphone amplified to the stage in the distance, and speakers along the last stretch of the route.

She turns to Tilly and Camas, "I woke up this morning and said to myself, it's a damn good day for a manifesto."

The crowd erupts in whoops, hollers and hoorays.

The president speaks confidently, reciting from memory. "I feel the power of my legs to carry me on this bicycle to smell the fresh air, to buy a sweet, crisp apple that fell from a tree a few miles from here, and to sit a spell with you."

The crowd and the riders recite passionately along with her.

"Today, with gyroscopic momentum, we roll across these paths and roads under our own power from the Pacific coast of Washington State to Washington DC on a bicycle."

Tilly and Camas look at each other with tears welling up in their eyes.

Mothers and fathers stand with children in the crowd.

"We ride for children making their way to school safely on bikes. We ride for my mother and father to ride a bicycle without fear of being crushed under the wheels of a passing truck."

Pedro barks, and the president waves him ahead. The bodyguards open up, and Liam and Pedro pedal to Tilly's side. Liam takes Tilly's hand for a moment and smiles.

There are many older, grey-haired people in the crowd and among the riders.

"We ride for our grandparents to ride to the market to buy vegetables for their supper, flowers for a neighbor, then safely home again."

A family rides their bikes on a country road near an oil drilling field in Texas.

"And during these times, as we ride side-by-side, the car in my garage is as old as me, and the clock will tick until soon the last pipeline full of gas, the last barrel of crude oil, and the last container of coal will leave our mother earth."

The president reaches the Lincoln Memorial, stops, and stands over her bike. She turns towards all of the riders behind her that fill the entire National Mall. All the people filling the mall, along with people across the country in living rooms watching TV, in cafes watching on their phones, stopped on their bikes commuting home, recite the final manifesto phrase.

"One city, one country, one continent, one planet united in abundance, peace, harmony, joy, laughter, and love by the world's greatest invention: the bicycle!"

CHAPTER 44

DOG BASKET: A BASKET DESIGNED TO CARRY SMALLER DOGS SAFELY ON THE BACK OF A BICYCLE

A na and Topper perform on a stage overlooking the beautiful Lincoln Memorial Reflection Pool. The Petal Pedal riders celebrate and dance throughout the National Mall. A large video screen on the stage shows the June 4th Bikes First commitment numbers scrolling up to ninety-seven percent, then still climbing, up, up, up. The screen changes color as it gets closer to the one hundred percent goal. Ana and Topper transform their music to a faster, frenetic, upbeat song with a drum roll in the background. They continue as the numbers climb. The screen turns green, followed by a screen of tulips and "100%!"

The crowd erupts in excitement with shouts, laughter, and applause. Tilly hugs Camas and Pedro, then kisses Liam. Ana kisses Topper. Camas and Tilly lift their watches to face the crowd to celebrate remotely with Max, Graeme, Bram, Mayor Pat, and Ella. The San Francisco, Napa, Sandglass, and Utrecht team members jump up and down in joyful delight.

Tilly and Liam walk along the reflection pool.

"I hope this hasn't totally messed up your training for the Finland race."

"I was thinking that I could train in that reflection pool," Liam jokes.

"You're very cute," Tilly says lovingly.

"I decided not to do Finland."

Tilly is surprised. "What? Why?"

"One reason is too much jet fuel. Someone I love has taught me about that."

"Awww," Tilly says, hugging him.

"And, we have an even better international race close by?"

"What race is that?"

"One that Camas and I are sponsoring on Lake Bijou Nez. The money is going towards the bike-city conversion in Sandglass. It's going to pay for the bike lane painting, road dividers, and bike education."

"So that's why Camas likes you now," Tilly says, smiling.

"When you told me she was a little jealous of Ana, I thought teaming up would be a good thing."

"You are a wise man. And handsome. And sexy. And..." Liam pulls her in and kisses her deeply.

Colorful sailboats can be seen in the distance on beautiful Lake Bijou Nez as swimmers register for the Sandglass Three Island Swim. Tilly and Graeme stand at the registration table, handing out registration packets. Camas struts confidently with a clipboard, flirting with the athlete swimmers.Liam walks to Tilly at the registration desk in wetsuit-shorts, shirtless. "Will you help me with my number, Miss," he says in an exaggerated baritone.

"Why, yes, I'd love you."

Tilly takes the sharpie, looks him in the eyes, bends down slowly to draw his number on his swim cap on the table. Liam admires her beauty.

"May I?" Tilly asks, provocatively, nodding to his shoulder.

"Yes, please," Liam responds.

Tilly slowly writes his number on his muscular, handsome shoulder. Liam closes his eyes, enjoying her touch. Tilly kisses him on the lips with his eyes closed. He opens them.

"Good luck, my love."

They embrace, and Liam runs off to the shoreline.

Camas counts down the start of the race on the loudspeaker. A loud bell starts the race. The swimmers run and dive into the water. White water erupts from the movement of the swimmers.

Camas let's out a loud "Whoop! Let's party!"

A band starts up on the lawn, and people begin to dance.

Costumed burners dance ecstatically in front of a fantastic light and art exhibit at Black Rock City. Tilly and Liam ride past on the tandem bicycle, dressed in extravagantly beautiful white costumes. They pass the elders' Moroccan tent and blow kisses to Max and Samprati standing outside the door of the tent. Graeme and Liz, in costume, follow on their bikes and wave to the Burning Man elders.

Camas follows skimpily clad on her lighted bike in a sexy, colorful, elaborate costume. "Boob wedding favors! Yes, these are my boobs. Boob wedding favors!" she calls as she hands out necklaces to the passers-by, stopping to hug them.

A *Just Married* sign hangs on the back of a tulip-decorated cargo trailer pulled by the tandem bike carrying Pedro wearing a white bandana. Pedro barks joyfully at the cans dragging on the ground behind.

THE END

PEDRO'S PRIMER

Tilly asked me to share a few woofs with you.

On that rare day you can't ride your bike, and there's no bike lane, will you please leave 3 feet between you and me in my bike trailer and have patience? When I get anxious to get to the dog park, Tilly tells me... "P, just breathe."

Please ride your bike as often as you can to reduce CO_2, that bad stuff eating away the snowcone layer and causing crazy thunder that scares me.

People think I chase cars because I'm not smart, but I'm running alongside to tell them,

"Ride a bike!"

P

PEDRO DE SOUSA SARAMAGO MEGELLAN

PREQUEL SHORT STORY

Go to www.AvisKalfsbeek.com/Max for the Prequel Short Story, Max's Holy Ride

EARLY CHAPTERS

Become a Patron for early chapters and books at www.patreon.com/pedrothewaterdog

AFTERWORD
THE MANIFESTO

"I feel the power of my legs to carry me on this bicycle to smell the fresh air, to buy a sweet, crisp apple that fell from a tree a few miles from here, and to sit a spell with you.

Today, with gyroscopic momentum, we roll across these paths and roads under our own power from the Pacific coast of Washington State to Washington DC on a bicycle.

We ride for children making their way to school safely on bikes.

We ride for my mother and father to ride a bicycle without fear of being crushed under the wheels of a passing truck.

We ride for our grandparents to ride to the market to buy vegetables for their supper, flowers for a neighbor, then safely home again.

And during these times, as we ride side-by-side, the car in my garage is as old as me, and the clock will tick until soon the last pipeline full of gas, the last barrel of crude oil, and the last container of coal will leave our mother earth.

One city, one country, one continent, one planet united in

abundance, peace, harmony, joy, laughter, and love by the world's greatest invention: the bicycle!"

Tilly DeMontagne and Camas

"Let me tell you what I think of bicycling. I think it has done more to emancipate women than anything else in the world. It gives women a feeling of freedom and self-reliance. I stand and rejoice every time I see a woman ride by on a wheel...the picture of free, untrammeled womanhood."

Susan B. Anthony